FASTBALL

A WILDE PLAYERS DIRTY ROMANCE

USA *Today* Bestselling Authors

A.M. HARGROVE
& TERRI E. LAINE

Cover by Michele Catalano - Creative

Cover photo by Sara Eirew

ISBN-13: 978-1537571409

ISBN: 1537571400

DEDICATION

This one is dedicated to women who love to watch hot men play sports and to the hot men who love to play them.

GINA

Air clings to my lungs like sludge, and the need to get out of here if I want to breathe becomes urgent. Without thinking, I make my way to the elevator in the skybox and am grateful when the doors whoosh open immediately after I press the button. I step inside, face forward, and press a lower floor button at random. That is when my eyes connect with his just as the doors silently shut between us. Exhaling a long breath, I'm grateful for the solitude. There is no reason on earth I should want the man. He's dangerous to my free-spirited lifestyle. Not to mention, he's too vanilla for my liking.

After the doors reopen, I don't recognize my location. When they start to shut, I leap out into the wide corridor, which is big enough for large vehicles to maneuver through. An underground tunnel of drab gray greets me. As I begin to walk, I realize I'm probably in a restricted area of the football stadium.

Fletcher Wilde, the star quarterback of the Oklahoma Rockets and my best friend, Cassidy's husband, is going to murder me if I get caught and they learn I'm a guest of his in the owner's box.

Feeling mischievous, my hesitant steps turn confident, figuring my bestie will talk her man off a rampage if he gets in trouble because of me. I pass several people but hold my head high and steady, acting as though I belong, and the people pass without a second glance. I cover my belly as if my stomach hurts, hiding the area where a badge might hang, which I suspect I need in order to be here.

The roar of the crowd funnels through a wide opening in the tunnel, and I can see the green of the field. I quickly dart past and stand near an open door. Just as I'm about to continue my exploration, a giant of a man steps in my path. He wears a sports coat that looks like the size of a tablecloth. But it's a walkie-talkie clipped to his shoulder with an attached coiled wire leading to his ear that explains his profession.

"Miss, do you have an ID?"

Busted. Fletcher's so going to kill me. "Um—"

"There you are." I turn to see Ryder striding in my direction.

"Hey, my cousin—"

"I know you," the guard says, with his index finger raised and pointing. His eyes are large. "You're Ryder Wilde. You play for the Charlotte Cougars. I watched you the other night. That triple saved the fucking game."

The security guy sees NFL players all the time, and yet he seems genuinely excited to meet Ryder. Just goes to show me what a big deal he is. Still, I'm surprised the guard is talking about Ryder's hitting skills, when normally it's all about his pitching capabilities.

Ryder grins, and they trade a secret male handshake all men seemed to know.

"Do you mind if I show her my cousin's locker?"

Ryder's and Fletcher's dads are brothers.

A wink and a nod, not to mention a trade of greenbacks, and the guard lets us by.

"We don't normally allow people into the locker room, especially during games. But for you, I'll give you ten minutes. Any more and someone is sure to come around and catch you," he calls over his shoulder.

"Thanks," Ryder says.

Then he's half-dragging me into what appears to be a fancy locker room. Two foot wide open lockers line the walls with benches in front of them. A wide-open space is in the middle, and several TVs grace the walls. The game is on in stereo. Two large empty dumpsters are nearby. I can only imagine them filled with sweaty uniforms to be laundered by unfortunate employees of their laundry service.

"So, are you going to tell me why I had to chase you?" Ryder begins.

The puff of air I release isn't filled with the heat of the dragon I'd felt minutes before. The man is too

3

beautiful to be angry at. Damn Wilde men.

"I didn't ask you to follow," I say.

"No, but your jealousy is obvious."

I roll my eyes in self-defense of his smirk. "Jealousy requires that I care and I don't." Which is such a lie. I'm surprised my nose doesn't grow two inches.

"Of course, you don't. I've called you for the past two months and nothing. I see you and you do everything possible to avoid me."

Wrapping an armor of nonchalance around me, I try to sound convincing when I speak again. "We had sex. It was good. I'm not interested in more. Isn't that a guy's wet dream to fuck and not worry about commitment?"

"I'm not most guys," he snaps, sounding offended I've lumped him in a category of cavemen. And maybe I have, because that I can handle.

"No, you are a guy on a date. One who should be upstairs with her and not with me."

He licks lips made for kissing as I watch him... them. *Damn* me. "You know what I think?"

"Not really," I say, feigning boredom. "But you're going to tell me, right?"

"I think you want me to fuck you again because you can't get enough. I think you're afraid you might get addicted to my dick."

"A-*DICK*-ted... I don't think so."

"Maybe you already are." His smug laugh is sexy as hell. *Double damn*.

"Try me. Fuck me right now and see if you can get

me off and have me begging for more."

Challenge issued. Will he take me up on it? Truth be told, the idea of fucking right out here in the open and potentially getting caught already has me wet.

"But what if we—" He glances around as if he hopes someone will appear.

"What are you, twelve and afraid we'll get caught by Mommy and Daddy?"

His head whips back in my direction, and his eyes grow stormy. Hot damn, he looks like a predator about to eat his prey, and I want him to do just that.

"Take your fucking jeans off, Gina," he commands.

The bass in his voice vibrates from his chest, sending shivers through me. I so want him that bad I easily comply. Although the denim peels off, they hook at my ankles, and I manage to only kick one leg off. He doesn't wait. I'm instantly lifted and set on the edge of the counter that's the perfect height for me to wrap my legs around him. He doesn't bother with my thong.

A dip of his hand into his front pocket, and he pulls out a condom.

"Expecting to get laid," I chide.

"Knowing," he says. Confidence exudes from him like cologne. "I put it in there on the ride down."

Fucking cocky bastard.

I watch as he sheathes the thick length of himself in the rubber wrapper. He's rough when he pokes a finger through my slit to test my readiness.

"What happened to Mr. Nice Guy?" I egg him on,

5

liking him crossing over to the dark side.

"You don't want nice. You want hard, fast, and meaningless. And I'm going to give it to you."

There's no time to gasp. He quickly removes his finger, shoves my thong to the side, and positions his tip at my entrance. He's inside me before I can blink. Damn, if I don't remember every inch of him. No man has fit me like a glove the way he does and ain't that a bitch. I've been waiting for him to strike out, and he's hit a goddamn homerun.

"Fuck," I cry out, not caring about the security guy at the door.

In fact, the idea that he may come in and watch has me tipping toward an edge sooner than I thought possible.

Ryder is relentless. He rides me so hard the back of my legs sting from the impact against the sharp edge they hang over. My eyes remain open and focused between us. I watch his cock slide in and out of me as the evidence of my pleasure coats each of his strokes. It's another shove closer to the cliff I desperately want to tumble over.

"I want you to swallow my dick and let my cum mark your throat."

Damn, if I don't scream from the impact of his hips as his rolls them so his dick hits that secret spot. Somehow knowing what I'm about to do, Ryder is there covering my mouth with his as he shoves his tongue to stop my sharp cries. Damn, if the fucker doesn't have to even touch my clit to set me off like a rocket launcher. I'm so confused as to how he managed it. Then again, I'm lost to the feeling of ecstasy as he grunts. His thrusts becoming bruising as he follows me into oblivion.

"So much for me deep-throating you," I tease once I'm able to catch my breath.

"There'll be a next time."

"That's what you think."

"Hey, you?" another voice declares.

I look over Ryder's shoulder and see a different guy, one not wearing a sports coat. So not security, but he's got on a polo shirt with Fletcher's team logo emblazoned on the breast pocket.

"Oh, are we in the wrong place?" Ryder says assuredly, not looking back.

He probably doesn't want the guy to recognize him.

"Yes, you are."

"Give me a minute for my girl to get decent."

Hearing him label me as his sends a thrill I don't want to run through me. I push down the feeling, knowing disappointment when he moves on will only leave me lonely. And everyone leaves me, even Cassidy. She's Fletcher's now, and I have no one left.

The man turns, giving us his back. "You have twenty seconds."

The threat is clear, and Ryder doesn't waste time. He helps me down, and he pulls up his jeans as I race to get mine on. And then we are running. We leave out a door closer to us and furthest from the guy who caught

7

us. Ryder reaches into his pocket and hands the security guy out front more money.

"Thanks," Ryder says. "Can you buy us some more time?"

He's got a fucking innocent face that makes everyone a believer. Then he adds a wink. Security guy smiles and nods, and then we are running.

Breathless from laughing so hard, we are in the elevator headed back up to the owner's box. When our laughter dies, Ryder crowds me in a corner. I don't fight when he kisses me. In fact, I rake my nails through his hair trying to pull him closer.

The elevator dings to signal we've made it to our floor. We break apart before the doors totally open, and a blond—not just anyone—is standing there looking at us.

"I was just looking for you," she says. And her saccharin sweet voice grates on my nerves. "I didn't know you had a girlfriend." Her pout belongs on the face of a five-year-old not a woman.

"Lynsey," he begins.

Meeting her eyes, I say, "Don't worry, honey. We aren't anything. In fact, he's all yours."

I stride away with my head held high. The prickle of guilt I feel is a useless emotion. I don't owe her anything. It was his choice to screw me. They aren't married, so what? But I know what it's like to be her, so that guilt still holds. But I've gotten my dose of Ryder. I hope that's enough for me to move on this time.

RYDER

hy the fuck did I have to bring Lynsey? If I could punch myself in the face for doing so, I probably would have right then. But instead, I paste on a paper-thin smile and drag my leaden feet out of the elevator.

"Where've you been? I've been looking all over for you."

Her voice, which at one point I thought sounded cute and sexy, now reminds me of fingernails on a blackboard. And that bleached out hair. What the fuck was I ever thinking? All I want right now is that hot black-haired wild thing wrapped around me again.

"Ryder? I asked you a question." Her bony arms wind around my neck as she shimmies her body close to mine. This used to be something that was a turn-on, but all I want to do is push her away from me.

Then she sounds like a damn Beagle as she starts to

sniff. Rising to her tippy toes, she puts her nose on my neck and sniffs some more. All of a sudden that cute little pout turns into a nasty sneer. "You were with her, and I'm talking with her with her, weren't you? That's why you were gone so long." Her voice has a high-pitched squeaky quality to it that is totally grating on my nerves. I need to calm her down before we walk back inside and she makes a scene, completely embarrassing Gina.

"Come on, Lynsey. Do you really think I'd do such a thing?"

She taps the toe of one of her stiletto boots as she assesses me. Who the hell wears these kinds of boots to a football game anyway? They look like they belong more on a stripper's pole. Then she crosses her arms, one of the little moves she loves because it squishes her manmade boobs together, giving her cleavage an extra oomph. The tight V-neck sweater she wears emphasizes them even more. The first time she did this I wanted to grab her tits and squeeze them, but this time I only want to tell her to stop it. It's not a very attractive move. It makes me think of Gina in her Oklahoma Rockets jersey and tight jeans. Now that's what I call sexy.

"I don't know, Ryder. Why do you smell like perfume? And Angel at that? It's one of my favorite scents, and I'm not wearing it today."

"I have been hugging a lot of women since I got here." I feel like a shit, even though there is no emotional attachment to this woman. The fact is, I should never have brought her. We've never been anything to each other but a date, even though she's wanted more. It's awkward and uncomfortable, but I didn't know Gina was going to be here. What is it with me? Can I not go anywhere alone?

She glares at me.

"Look, I want to catch the game, and I can't do it standing out here. You coming inside or not?"

"Maybe I should just go."

"Suit yourself."

A huff rushes out of her. "You mean you're gonna let me leave by myself?"

"Of course not. I'll order an Uber for you."

Her mouth flaps open and closed a couple of times, and then she says, "Fine. Why don't you do that?"

I yank out my phone and tap on the Uber app, praying they come to the correct entrance of the stadium. It says they'll be here in five minutes. I imagine they are circling the place like buzzards. They probably make a killing on game day.

"Let's go. Your ride will be here in five."

The walk down is in complete silence. I believe Lynsey is as done with me as I am with her. By the time we get to the doors, her ride is waiting. Now for the awkward part.

"Take care, Lynsey."

"Like you care, Ryder."

"What? It's not like that."

But isn't it?

11

"I may look it, but I'm not stupid. See ya." She holds up her hand over her shoulder as she sashays to the car, flicking her fingers, telling me goodbye.

I jog back to the box, hoping to see Fletcher in at least one play before halftime. But as I burst into the room, I see all the players moving off the field. *Dammit!*

Everyone ambles toward the buffet or bar to refresh their food and drink. Cassidy and my twin sister, Riley, approach, so I know I'll be on trial.

Riley's eyes range up and down my body. I hate it when she does this. It always makes me want to squirm.

"What?" I ask her.

"Where's Lynsey?"

"She left."

"Left?" Riley asks.

"Yeah, she didn't want to watch the game after all."

It's funny seeing both sets of brows shoot straight up in synchronized timing. I'd like to ask if they planned it, but I'm damn sure they'd punch me. Or something equally as painful.

Leave it to Riley to keep digging in. "So what? Did she like decide after she'd been here a while, and mind you this wasn't her first game, that she didn't like football after all?"

"Something like that," I mumble.

"Ryder, what did you do?"

"Nothing." *If only they knew.*

They share a look, and those damn brows of theirs arch again. I wonder if they're on some kind of team.

Synchronized brow raising team. Maybe it's some club only women are allowed in.

"Whatever," Riley finally answers.

They both turn and leave. Funny. Cassidy never said a word. Only listened to our exchange. Too bad I can't pull her aside and drill her with questions about Gina. That wouldn't work though because it would only get back to that dark-haired vixen who's gotten under my skin.

Speaking of, where the hell is she? I do a once-over in the room, and there are so many people in here it's difficult to see who's who. Looks like I'm going to have to mingle to find her.

People stop to congratulate me on the win yesterday, which was why I didn't get here until late today. And I have to ask myself again. Why the hell did I ask Lynsey to meet me? What a huge mistake. My hand swipes through my hair as I continue my search for Gina.

"Ryder? There you are. I was wondering where you went."

"Hey, Mom."

"Where's Lynsey?"

"She left. She decided she wanted to go home."

"Well, I'm glad. I don't really like that woman. Seems to me she only wants what you can buy her. Did you eat, honey?"

"Not yet."

She grabs my hand and pulls me over to the food table, like I'm eight years old. I love my mother. She's the

13

most adorable woman in the world. She's kind and loving, but right now I want to find that fiery little piece that nearly blew my mind a few minutes ago.

"Let me fix you a plate." She starts piling food on so there's no way I'm getting out of this. She stuffs it in my hands and says, "I'll grab you a beer, sweetie."

"Thanks, Mom. But you know I am twenty-six and I can fix my own plate."

"I know, honey but you know how I love to take care of you."

I scan the place for an empty seat and find one toward the corner. I turn back and say, "Mom, I'll be over there."

"Okay, honey, I'll find you."

As I walk, I check out the goodies Mom placed on my plate, and my stomach rumbles. It smells delicious, and I'm starving. Sitting down, I dig in and Mom hands me my beer and leaves with an *I'll be back with dessert.* As I inhale my food, a sexy voice filled with sarcasm comes from over my shoulder.

"By the looks of it, someone needs to make sure you, um, eat more." My beer spills on my lap as I nearly choke.

"Jesus, are you okay?"

After I cough and sputter a bit, I say, "Yeah, I think I'll live. Don't you know it's not safe to sneak up on people while they're eating?"

Gina gives me an eat shit look and shakes her head. Black shiny waves swing back and forth, and her scent drifts over me. My cock instantly strains against my jeans. I want to pull her down on top of me and push myself into her until she moans. *What the fuck, Ryder?*

"You okay there?" she asks.

"Yeah, why?"

"You were licking your lips like you tasted something out of this world."

"Well, I was just eating," I say, adding, "until you about choked me."

"Right." She drags the word out, making it sound as though she believes me as much as she believes cows can fly.

To take my mind off of sex, I shove a huge forkful of food into my mouth. And chew. And chew. And chew. I don't think I'm ever going to work that mouthful down, but I do. And the entire time I feel Gina's heat behind me.

"So, where's the blond?" she finally asks. I knew it was coming, but now it's out in the open.

After swallowing my food, I say, "She left. Why don't you come over here and sit next to me so I don't have to strain my neck to talk and I won't be concerned about choking again?"

She shrugs a shoulder and moves next to me. "Did I get you in trouble?"

"No, Gina, I got myself in trouble. I should never have brought her. It was a huge error."

She sips on her drink. "Because of me?"

"Yes, because of you. I bring her and disappear with

you."

"Well, she didn't have to leave because of me. I meant what I said to her. You and I aren't anything, so it isn't a big deal."

This is weird. She acts like a guy. Women don't act like this. She's supposed to be more clingy since we just fucked a few minutes or so ago.

"Why are you acting like this?" I ask.

"Acting like what?"

Setting the food to the side, I turn to look her square in the face. "Like this. We just had sex."

"Will you keep it down, for Christ's sake? You want to tell the world?"

Damn, this woman is so hot when she's angry. Two spots of color appear high on her cheekbones as her nostrils flare. Eyes like coffee make me want to dive right into them and drink them up. She's as perfect as I've ever seen a woman be with her waist long shiny hair, and she's tall—my guess is about five feet nine or ten—and that's a huge turn-on for me alone. But the best thing is, she's not bone thin like so many women are. She's got curves in all the right places and knows what to do with them.

"No one is paying us a bit of attention."

She licks her full lips—the very same ones I want wrapped around my dick—and says, "Well, they will be if you keep shouting about us having sex."

I laugh at this. Is this the same woman who challenged me in the locker room? Now she's afraid someone will hear about it when a few minutes ago, she didn't give a fuck if someone caught us doing it.

"What?" she asks.

"You're impossible."

"How so?"

I tell her what a contradiction she is, and she actually has the courtesy to blush before she speaks again. "Well, that was different."

"No, it wasn't. What if I slipped my hand down your pants right here, in this room, and got you off?"

Her eyes dart around as she checks out the room. An impish look takes over her face, and she says, "Okay."

Jesus, I was only joking, and here she is taking me seriously.

"Okay, but here's the deal. You have to return the favor."

She holds out her hand and says, "Deal."

After we shake on it, she undoes her pants and covers her fly with her jersey.

"How quiet can you be?" I ask.

"Very."

"Hmm. We'll see about that."

The bad thing about this is Gina has a gorgeous pussy, and I want to look at it, but unfortunately, I'm left with my imagination. Instead, I focus on her eyes. Using one hand for obvious reasons, my fingers spread her lips, and I begin a slow rub until she warms to me. It doesn't take her long I'm happy to say. One finger in and she's wiggling around in her seat.

"Be still," I warn.

"Trying here," she breathes heavily.

Using two fingers and my thumb, I massage her, pressing down on her pubic bone with the heel of my palm.

"Shit, that's good," she whispers.

"Ryder, here's your dessert, honey."

Fuck! My mom would have to come right now.

"Gina, honey, would you like me to get you some?"

"No, ma'am, I'm fine." Her voice breaks as she speaks, and I have to hold back a laugh.

"Oh, dear, you're a bit sweaty. Are you okay? You're not getting sick, are you?"

"No, ma'am, I'm fine. These games always get me a little worked up."

"Ryder, aren't you going to eat your dessert?"

I'm holding the plate with one hand, and the other is in Gina's vag.

"Yeah, I will, Mom."

"Here," Gina says, coming to my rescue. "I think I'll have one bite if you don't mind."

She takes a bite and gives me one.

"Ryder, you let these women spoil you too much. I'm going to find your dad."

When her back is to us, I resume my ministrations on Gina's privates. But I go in for the money without mercy. In no time flat she's clenching my fingers as she comes all around my hand. And she was wrong. She moans. Loud enough so she puts the plate down and clamps a hand over her mouth.

Then we laugh as I remove my hand and lick my fingers. "I believe this is my dessert."

"Oh yeah?"

"Uh huh," I mumble.

"My turn."

"God, I hope Mom doesn't come back. Where's that dessert? If I don't eat it, she'll think I'm sick."

Gina hands me the plate, and I eat the cake or whatever it is that's there. I feel her hands trying to unbutton my pants.

"You can't do this," I scold her.

"Why not?"

"Because we're in the box with people around."

"So?" She looks as though it's an everyday occurrence.

"How many times have you done this?" I ask.

Her lip pokes out, and she says, "You're not supposed to ask those kinds of questions, Ryder."

"I don't have a shirt on like you do to cover myself. I don't want my dick exposed to the world while you give me a hand job."

She smirks. "You're a chicken."

"Yeah, I am."

She points a finger at the plate and says, "Finish up there, my little chicken."

Who am I to disobey an adventurous woman? When I'm done, I set the plate aside, and she takes my hand, pulling me into the bathroom in the back of the room.

"Ahh, good idea," I say as she locks the door.

By this time, my dick is about to tear through the zipper. She undoes it and pulls it free of the jail it's been in. Then I watch in wonder as she drops to her knees and puts her lips around the tip, sucking me into the warmth of her mouth.

It's about now that I want to moan my pleasure, but I stay quiet. Watching Gina with my cock in her mouth is quite the picture. She takes me in a little deeper each time, and she watches me—she fucking watches me. It makes me want to fuck her hard, like I did earlier. But I also want to come on her tongue, down her throat. I want to feel her swallow what I pump into her, squeezing me until I'm dry. The way she swirls her tongue around my head and then slides it along my shaft almost has me unglued. But then she takes me in deeper than I think is possible, squeezing my balls until I tell her, letting her know I'm close. And that's when she really goes at it until I shoot everything I have into her. And I, exactly like she did, have to hold a hand over my mouth to stop the groan from escaping.

As soon as possible, I tuck my dick back in my jeans and zip up.

"Let's go," I say.

And when I open the door, Cassidy and Riley stand there staring at us.

GINA

Pushing my hair back, I smirk at Cassie and walk past with my head held high. So I sucked Ryder off in the bathroom. It was fucking hot. The guy pushes all my buttons. If anything, I should be more wary of that.

Heading for the bar, I ask for a shot of tequila. Before I know it, I'm cornered by Cassie and Riley.

"So, are you going to tell us what you were doing in the bathroom with Ryder?" Cassie tosses out.

"And let's just put it out there. Are you fucking my brother?" Riley asks, double teaming me.

I'm not a blusher, because rarely do I ever give a crap about what people think of me. But I've never been ambushed by a sister.

Pulling up my metaphorical big girl pants, I say, "You want to know what I was doing in the bathroom?" They both nod. "I was doing him. So what? Neither one of you is our mother."

I start to walk away, but Riley brings me up short.

"Just some friendly advice, because I think you and I could be fast friends, but a bit of a warning, too. My brother is a lover. You know what I mean? He loves women, hard and fast and more times than I can count. But on the same note, he's a Wilde. You remember that conversation we had before? When he loves, he loves hard and long. And can be hurt. Don't hurt my brother."

The warning is received. She feels for Ryder like I feel for Cassie. She may not be my blood sister, but that doesn't stop the bond we formed over many years of taking care of one another.

"I doubt I could. Besides, I like it hard and fast, too," I say cheekily. "I'm not the lover type, so no worries there."

Cassie sees through my shit. She gives me a sideways glance, but thank goodness she doesn't give up the goods in front of Ryder's sister.

"Good. Then we won't have a problem. Besides, I truly think he's into someone, so it's a good thing you're not a clinger," Riley says.

The comment hurts, and it shouldn't. I brush it aside and smile.

"So not a clinger," I say, waving a hand.

Then I spot Ryder talking to a very cute perky woman who must have something in her eye the way she's batting her eyelashes at him.

"We should hang out sometime. I don't know anybody," Riley is saying, so I turn my attention back to them.

"Abso-fucking-lutely. I know a club we can go to."

Cassie jumps in. "You are not taking her to a sex club."

"Why the fuck not? It's not like I do anything there besides watch. It's fun. Plus, you can find guys that aren't looking for the long-term," I protest.

"There are plenty of guys in normal clubs for that. You should go out with Mark."

I feel like I bit into a lemon as a sour taste fills my mouth because he's like a brother to me.

Riley says with clappy hands, "Mark who?"

"Mark, Fletcher's best friend." Something crosses over Riley's face, but I continue, "And don't get me wrong. He's easy to gaze at, but he's too vanilla for me."

"That's not what you said," Cassie teases.

"Oh, my, god. We were in high school. He was my first," I explain to Riley. "But soon we realized we worked better as friends."

Cassie's eyes sparkle with something like a matchmaker's twinkle. "I could introduce you."

I put a hand up. "Let me stop this train from shooting down the tracks. I think Riley's more like me than you and Fletcher. Mark is too romantic for her."

"Yes, you have my number. So Mark's out. But I've never been to a sex club. Sounds like fun and, Cassie, you have to go with."

"Oh, I so will not," Cassie says.

In agreement with Riley, I say, "Yes, my bestie, you will have to come."

"Fletcher would just die," she says.

"There's no law against just looking, Cassie. Besides, if he truly loves you, he has to trust you completely."

Cassie can't say anything.

After the game, I'm sorry I brought it up. Fletcher and Cassie get into a bit of an argument over the topic of her hanging out with me at the club. I try to butt in, but Fletcher does that growly thing for me to stay out of it.

Mark leans over. "Sex club, huh?"

Our long ago, very short-lived relationship isn't a problem for either of us. He's like my brother now.

Shrugging, I say, "It's something to do."

"Have you ever participated?" he asks mischievously.

"No." I'd thought about it. But it's one thing to play games behind the closed doors of your house, and it's another to have the idea that you might get caught doing things. It's a whole different thing to actually be on display. Even I'm not that bold.

"You are being safe, right?" Mark asks, taking my hand in his.

"I am." I squeeze his in mine.

"You know I'm only thirty minutes and a phone call away if you ever need me."

"I know," I say. "How about you? Are you seeing anyone?" The smile shoots to his eyes, so there is someone special. "Who is she?"

Using his other hand, he brushes a finger down my nose. "You know I don't kiss and tell. If things get serious, you'll be the first to meet her and my litmus test."

When we make it to Fletcher's mini mansion, not small my ass as Cassie claimed, the pair have made up. It's almost gross to watch them play grabby hands as they practically race to their bedroom.

"Are you going to bed?" Mark asks when we're left alone.

"In a few."

"If you're not ready to head to bed, do you want company?" I shake my head. "All right, I'm going to bed then."

"You're going to call that girl and have phone sex, aren't you?"

The smile he shines on me is so bright, I have to raise a hand to block it. I swat at him, and he dodges before heading to his assigned room upstairs.

Alone, I pour a drink and stare at myself in the mirror. I hate the woman who stares back at me. And not that I hate myself. But I'm the spitting image of my mother, or so I'm told, a woman I never knew.

Pushing back the mass of black hair, I wish I had the guts to cut it all off or bleach it. That way maybe I wouldn't look so much like the tourist girl who'd come to the mountains with her family so many years ago. She saw my father and had to have him, if you believe the stories he tells. She got herself knocked up and nearly disowned. When I was born, she dropped me off at my dad's parents' house and never looked back.

He didn't even know her last name, their relationship was so *wham bam thank you ma'am*. I grew up with a dad who was way too young to want to be a father and grandparents way too old to be parents. Somehow in between I'd managed, thanks to Cassie and her family.

"What are you thinking about?"

I turn, nearly swallowing my tongue out of fright, not knowing someone was downstairs with me.

"What are you doing here?" I ask instead.

"I didn't want to stay at the hotel with my sister and parents. And Fletcher's my cousin. I've stayed here several times. I have a key."

Holding it up, he gives me an impish grin.

Downing the contents of my glass, I set it on the bar, prepared to leave.

"So, are you a runner?"

Mystified, I turn to face the man. He takes off his baseball hat, which is perpetually on his head, and runs a hand through his dark hair. I stare at the arm sleeve. His tats make him appear more dangerous and the reason why I'd been so attracted to him when I spotted him that first time. I've always been a fan of a bad boy, which is why I never expected or wanted relationships to last. When he puts the hat back on, it's turned backwards, and damn, if that isn't sexy as fuck.

"Well," he says, reminding me I haven't answered his question.

"I've been known to jog a few times, why?"

When he smiles, a tiny perfect dimple appears on his cheek. "That's not what I mean. I think you're running from me. Why, I don't know."

"I'm not running from you," I deny it even though the truth is, I am. "I told you. I'm not into the relationship thing. We had a fun night, but that's it."

"What scares you about a relationship?"

This is a simple answer. I don't even have to think about it. "Let's see. My mom abandoned me as a child. My dad is the biggest manwhore alive. And honestly, I think I stand up for women by not being like all those whiny ones who played mommy to me until my dad got bored. And then they would cry and beg to be treated like shit. I want to be the opposite of them. I don't need a man to survive."

Ryder's brows shoot up, and I realize I may have said that with too much vehemence.

"Okay," he says, looking a little shell-shocked. "I didn't want to walk you down the aisle or anything. I just thought we could have fun together. And isn't it safer to have fun with one person?"

"Safe physically to be monogamous if both parties are and come into the arrangement clean."

"I'm clean. I'm tested all the time."

Shit, my brain. I hadn't meant to speak out loud, because it wasn't safer for my heart.

"Besides, you're a bit too vanilla for me anyway."

His eyes become the size of baseballs. "Vanilla? What? Are you into kinky shit?" He studies my eyes. "So it is true. You want to take Cassidy to a sex club."

"See, this is what I'm talking about. You're vanilla, and I'm not."

"But—"

"Don't bother. You have a small mind for a guy with a decent sized dick. Sex clubs are a place of acceptance for lovers of fucking. I go there and I'm not accused of being a slut because I like sex. I can find a partner that knows exactly what I need and isn't looking for a white picket fence and crumb snatchers. Don't get me wrong. I think that's great for some people. And kids are cute. But that's not what I'm looking for right now. And what the fuck? Just because I'm not a guy, I'm not allowed to enjoy myself in the company of men?"

"Wait—"

My regurgitation of my views leaves me feeling somewhat vindicated and hollow at the same time, so I leave while I'm ahead. I shut myself in my room and am grateful that all the bedrooms in the house have their own attached bath. I take a lingering shower, somewhat sad as I wash away Ryder's scent. I barely sleep, and then I'm out of the house before dawn, catching the Uber I'd set up. Some of us have to work to pay our bills. And when I get on the plane, I hope I don't cross paths with the guy who's too perfect for my cloud-covered future. I need distance from the man who makes vanilla seem a little spicy.

RYDER

You're a bit too vanilla for me. The phrase repeats itself in my head. And the bad thing is, I keep seeing her gorgeous mouth form the words, like a bad pitch on instant replay, over and over. What she doesn't know, didn't give me a chance to tell her, is I'd try anything with her—go to her sex club, venture out of my so-called *vanilla* lifestyle, and add in some kinky fucking if she wants. Hell, I'm all on board for that kind of shit. But no, she walks out, and won't answer my knocks on her bedroom door.

In the morning when I wander into the kitchen and ask about her, Fletcher tells me she's gone. She fucking left without a word. She pulled a goddamn man's move on me. And now I feel like a fucking pansy ass, with my balls crawling right up in my ass, quivering. Jesus, what is happening here? I don't normally fall this fast for a girl. But this time, she's nailed me but good. The thing is, I want her. I want more of Gina Ferraro.

"Coffee?" Fletcher's voice snags me out of my daydreams.

"Huh?"

"I asked if you wanted any coffee?" He holds up the pot and a mug.

"I guess so."

He pours while I watch. "Cream? Sugar? I can never remember."

"No."

"Eggs? Sausage? Bacon? Toast? It's all over there. Cass already cooked."

His words slip right past me as I stare into the dark contents of my mug.

"Ryder?" His voiced has an edge of annoyance to it.

"What?" I snap.

"Damn. What has you so grouchy this morning? You won't even answer any of my questions."

"Oh. Sorry. What did you say?"

He points to the counter and says, "Cassidy went to the trouble of cooking breakfast for everyone. Have the courtesy of thanking her even if you don't want any eggs, bacon, sausage, or toast."

Lifting my head, I notice the spread of food. "Fuck. Sorry, man." Then I hunt for Cassie and see her sitting at the table with Mark. I must look like the biggest douceface. "Thanks, Cassie. I appreciate it. Morning, Mark." I drag my ass over to the food and fill up a plate because I am starving, actually.

When I sit back down, I dive in and the breakfast is

fantastic. "Damn, this is great." Fletcher looks on with a smirk.

"Didn't know Cass was a superb cook, did you?"

"Had no clue," I say around a mouthful of eggs. "Excellent eggs here."

"You'd better slow it down, Ryder, or you're going to choke," Cassidy calls out from the table with a grin.

My plate is polished off, and I'm up for seconds. As I'm going in for the refill, I ask, "How many eggs did you cook?"

She says, "A cool dozen and a half. Fletcher can eat eight on his own if I don't make anything else to go with them."

"Yeah, especially during the season. I'm always hungry," Fletcher says.

"I'm the same way. A bottomless pit. But I don't have a wife that cooks hanging around."

"I don't either. Don't forget Cass isn't always here."

"You poor fucker. Tears are flowing. Boo-fucking-hoo."

Cassidy laughs along with Mark, and Fletcher flips me off.

"So, what crawled up your ass when you woke up? Was it the fact that some dark-haired little fireball wasn't around this morning?"

"Shut the hell up." I'm not going anywhere near the Gina topic with him or Cassidy, especially with Mark sitting here. He and Gina are close, not as close as Cassidy is to her, but I don't want Mark to go blabbing back to her about me.

"Oh, come on, Ryder. You know I won't say anything."

"Dude, you're married to her best friend. What the fuck!"

We both turn to Cassidy, and she has this super secretive look in her eyes that has me wanting to interrogate her for more information.

But Fletcher beats me to it. "What do you know that you aren't telling?" he asks.

"Nothing. But if I did, I wouldn't share anyway. Like Ryder said, I'm her bestie. My lips are sealed. And I'm talking super glued."

"Women. You always stick together," Fletch says with a chuckle.

Cassidy gets up and moves next to him. "You love it. Look what it did for us."

"Yeah, look."

Then they start to fucking make out like teenagers, and I want to puke up my breakfast. Good God, didn't anyone tell them that it was rude to show too much PDA? I look over at Mark and make a gag face. He laughs.

"Cut it out, you two," I finally say.

Fletch pulls his mouth off her with a pop and says, "I'm not sorry, man. I don't get enough of her since we live apart during the week."

"Yeah, yeah, yeah. I gotta go shower and get ready for my flight."

Six hours later, my plane lands in Charlotte. I can't

say I'm happy to be home, but maybe going back to work will take my mind off things. I keep staring at the tiny piece of paper that Cassidy pressed into my hand right before I left. All it said was *Whips And Cuffs—Asheville.* My thoughts are that this must be the sex club Gina frequents sometimes. Maybe Cassidy was trying to point me in this direction. Whatever. The problem is, I have to wait until the weekend since it's about a two and a half hour drive from here. This weekend would work since we don't have any games, but it's anyone's guess if Gina will be there. I might have to get some help from Cassidy or Fletcher if I'm going to make this work. In the meantime, maybe I can get Riley to ask Gina to one of my games.

When I get to my condo downtown, one of my teammates is crashed there.

"What the hell, Robinson?" I say. "I didn't give you a key so you could move in here."

He hangs his head and looks like hell. "Sorry, man. My wife kicked me out."

"Aw, fuck. What happened?"

"She caught me with that cheerleader."

I could kick his ass. He has the sweetest wife of any of the guys on the team. "Listen, dude. I hate to say this, but you deserve it. You know how I feel about Kristie. I love that woman of yours. Why the hell did you fuck around on her?"

He rubs his face, shaking his head. "I know. I royally screwed up, man. What am I gonna do?"

"Suck it up and do whatever it is she wants."

"That's just it, man. She won't even talk to me."

"So what went down?" I ask.

"We were all at the team picnic. You know which one? It's the one you missed. But, yeah, Delilah shows up and pulls me behind this building and starts blowing me."

"So, Robbie, what you're saying is she gave you absolutely no chance of saying—Gee, my wife, Kristie, is right over there, and I don't think this is very appropriate. Not to mention I love my wife?"

"I know, man. I suck."

"No, Delilah does."

He grins and says, "Man, does she ever. Like a fucking Dyson."

"Dammit, Rob! Get your shit straight here!"

"Okay, okay! So yeah, that's what happened, and I must've been gone too long or maybe it was the groans or something, but Kristie came a looking and there we were, me standing there with my cock and balls deep in Delilah's throat."

"Is that it?" I asked the question as a joke, but there was more.

"No, she had her finger up my ass, too."

"You have shit for brains, Robinson. End of story. Find a good lawyer. That's my advice. And I hope you lose your ass because you deserve it. Sorry. Not sorry." I get ready to walk to my room, but then say, "Oh, I need my key back. You can't stay here. You know my sister lives here now, and this won't work. Besides, if she finds out what you did to Kristie, she'll kick your ass all the way to the moon."

The look on his face is priceless. Jaw slack and hanging open, eyes wide—hell, if I didn't know better myself, I'd think he was getting sucked off right now. I hold my hand out waiting for said key. He digs in his pocket, pulls out his key chain, and struggles to get it off the ring.

"Can I stay here tonight?"

"Yeah, because Riley's out of town, but after that, you need to make other arrangements. And for the love of God, stay away from women for the time being." It's hard to believe someone can be that stupid. That's when I decide I'll never commit to a woman until I know with absolute certainty that she's *the one.*

Dropping my duffle in my room, I pick up my phone and call Riley.

"Hey, sis, I need your help. Can you bring Gina to a game with you?"

"Being that I'm in California right now, I don't think that's going to work."

"I don't mean today, smartass. I mean like the weekend after next."

"Why Gina?" She wants to know.

"Why not Gina?"

"I dunno. Just curious."

"She's fun, not to mention hot," I say. "Can you do it?"

"I'll ask. Just beware. She's not the settling down type."

A gust of laughter bursts from within me. "What the hell, Ri? Who said anything about settling down? I just want to get to know her a little better so maybe I can ask her out."

"Well, you already fucked her, so don't you know her well enough?"

"Wow. That's a bit harsh, isn't it? Don't you like her?"

"I do. Just being cautious for you, bro."

I pause a moment. "Since when have you been so protective of me?" I ask.

She quiets. "Okay, I'll ask. But if anything goes down that isn't good between you two, don't blame it on me."

"Why the hell would I do that?"

"And don't put me in the middle. I want to be her friend, you know?"

"Okay, okay. Gotcha. Just let me know a good day for you two. And thanks, Ri."

"You got it."

After we end the call, I think about how weird it all was. It almost sounded like Riley was jealous of me being with Gina. Like she wanted to be her friend only. She's never done that before, so why now? Maybe I'm just imagining things.

Next on my list is to google that sex club. I need to find out all about it. Maybe I'll take a trip there myself this weekend if I have the opportunity. Check things out, see what it's all about. I'm sure one of the guys would be happy to go with me. Who in their right mind wouldn't want to watch people having sex out in the open?

When I pull it up online, it looks a lot classier than I imagined. The best thing about it is you have to sign an NDA when you enter and no cameras or phones are allowed inside. That's good for me. I wouldn't want my picture to show up online in connection with a sex club. Wouldn't be good for my reputation.

The next day at practice, I hit up one of my teammates, David Lester—a third baseman, to see if he wants to head over to Asheville for the weekend.

"What's all the way in Asheville?" David asks.

"You know, it's cooler since it's up in the mountains. The leaves might be starting to change colors since fall's here, and I want to check out this cool club I've been hearing about. There are supposed to be some hot women who go there."

"I'm in."

"Great. We'll leave Saturday late afternoon since we don't have a game."

"Sounds good. Do you want to get us reservations someplace to stay overnight?" he asks.

"Yeah, I'll take care of it."

That night I make reservations at The Grove Park Inn, which is an old yet exclusive hotel that is close to the club.

On Saturday, we hit the road, and David talks nonstop. I swear, he's part woman. He's worse than my sister. The only thing he gives me a chance to say is, "Uh huh." He gives me the rundown on everything from the new boxer briefs he bought online to the car he's thinking about buying for his sweet grandmother who lives outside of some small town in the middle of a cornfield in Indiana.

"You wouldn't believe the corn there, man. It's the best tasting stuff you've ever had."

"Uh huh."

"Next time I go up in the summer, I'll bring you back a dozen or two ears."

"Uh huh."

"Hey, so ..."

I'm never so happy to see the entrance to a hotel in my life, as I am to see The Grove Park Inn. "Let's say we get checked in and then grab some dinner here. Then maybe head out around nine. You good with that?" I ask.

"Sure. Are there any cool tours we can take while we're here?" he asks.

"Tours. Tonight?"

"Yeah. Like, is there any kind of specialties here or anything? Like country basket weaving or pipe making?"

"What the fuck! We're not at Dollywood. But the Sierra Nevada Brewing Company has tours. That's pretty cool."

"Nah, I'm more interested in the local flavor."

"So, you'd rather watch someone weave baskets instead of touring a brewery? What kind of a man are you?"

David is a big guy. He shrugs his hugely defined shoulders, and they stretch the fabric of the shirt he wears. "I kinda like the homey stuff. I'm like that. Thought maybe there was somewhere they made corn pipes around here."

Corn pipes? Who the hell is this guy?

"Dude, I grew up in California, surfing and playing baseball, and only came to visit my cousins here, so I don't know too much about corn pipes." Now I'm wondering what good ol' David is going to think when I take him into Whips and Cuffs. Maybe I should've looked for a club called Corn Liquor and Porch Swings instead.

We meet for drinks and dinner, and one thing about David is he loves his brown liquor. Jack on the rocks. That probably should've told me a little about him. After we finish up, David's downed four or maybe five drinks and is feeling rather good. Time to Uber it over to the club because it's past nine. I don't want to be the first one there, but I don't want to go if it gets too crowded to get in either.

Our ride pulls into the parking lot and there's no sign, so I ask to make sure we're in the right place.

"So, I can guess you've never been here?" he asks.

"Never," I answer.

A hearty laugh rips out of him. "Have fun, gents," he says as we get out of the car. We can hear him laughing even as the car is a block away.

"What was that all about?" David asks.

"I don't know."

"What's the name of this place anyway?" he asks.

"Whips and Cuffs," I mumble as I take giant strides toward the entrance.

"I didn't get that," I hear him yell from over my shoulder, but I ignore him as I walk through the door.

The entrance is a dimly lit foyer with three huge bouncers guarding the second door.

"Welcome. Returning or new?" one of the giants asks. I'm a fairly tall guy at six feet four inches, and I have to tilt my head up to see his eyes. Good thing he doesn't recognize me. For once I'm glad someone isn't into baseball.

"New."

By this time, David is right behind me.

"He with you?"

"Yeah."

"Okay. Here are the rules. You must sign an NDA. Anyone you see inside, you must not speak of outside of this place. If they do not acknowledge you, you cannot speak to them here. Clear so far?"

"Yes."

The guy is silent. I turn to see what's happening with David and he's staring at the guy. I nudge him with my elbow. "Oh, yeah. Clear," he says.

"Good. Next, absolutely no pictures. Are you carrying?"

"Guns?" I ask.

He huffs out a breath. "Phones or cameras of any kind," he answers with great disdain. Then he points with his thumb over his shoulder and says, "The guy behind me is gonna pat you down and check for weapons."

"Oh, damn. I have my phone. David?"

"Yeah, I have a phone."

"We'll have to check those for you, and you can get them when you leave. If that's a problem, then you can't get in."

"Not a problem for me. David?"

"No problem."

"Finally, anything you see in here, you must not discuss outside of this club. Clear? If you do, you will be in violation of this NDA."

"Okay," I say.

He pulls out the NDA, and we both sign. He gives us copies and says that he'll check them with our phones, and we can get them when we leave. Then he hands us a little ticket stub. After that, we pay a fifty-dollar entrance fee, and he puts a band around our wrist.

The guy waits for us and does a quick check for weapons, and then allows us to enter when we pass.

We walk through another door, and it leads us to an elevator. We get on and take it down to the lower level.

"What the hell kind of place is this, Wilde? I've never gone to a club that required me to sign an NDA before. Or made me check my phone and get patted down for guns."

"Yeah well, it's a …" I don't get the chance to finish because the elevator doors open, and the explanation is right before us as we stand there. There are men and women who are either cuffed or tied while they are being sucked or fucked. There are all kinds of apparatuses everywhere, giant crosses tilted to stand in Xs, leather benches, and just about anyone one could imagine or beyond. Women and men run the gamut from being fully clothed to completely naked, and there's no use trying to disguise my astonishment or fascination with the place.

And then, there's David's reaction. "Well, I'll be damned. You never told me you were this kind of hound. No wonder you didn't want to take me on any tours. This puts a whole new spin on Dolly's Wood!" And then he lets out a very loud *Yahoo* that has lots of heads turning in our direction.

I thought I was prepared for this, that I was an adventurous sort. Boy was I wrong. This is so out of my league. There are people having sex in cages suspended from the ceiling. They are fucking against the wall hanging on to leather straps, banging it out in these little see-through cubicles, fucking doggie style over leather benches, women blowing men, men eating women, you name it. There are all kinds of apparatuses on which people are tied, hanging, swinging, flying even, and the thing is, everyone seems to be having a blast. But I feel like the only kid who has been left out of the secret.

And then I think of Gina coming here. Is this what she likes? Does she do it here? With people watching her? Am I even capable of this? Would I be willing to give it a try?

As I gaze around, David looks like that kid who only now discovered that women have tits. My God, he's loving this. I, on the other hand, am not sure of what to do, how to act.

"First time, huh?" A voice hits me in my ear.

"Uh, yeah."

"I was like that, too."

I look at the woman speaking. She's of medium height and semi-attractive.

"Someone I'm interested in comes here so I thought I'd check it out," I say.

"You're just shocked, but once that wears off, you'll be intrigued. Don't give up." She wanders off, and I keep thinking of Gina. *You're a bit too vanilla for me.* Her words nail me, and I realize then that I'd love to watch her in here unobserved. See how she really acts, uninhibited. See the real Gina behind the woman she shows me. My vanilla is tossed aside as the idea of that just creates the biggest boner, and I'm going to have to deal with it for the rest of the night, in a sex club no less. But fuck that. Vanilla Ryder is a thing of the past. From now on, I'm going to be raunchy Ryder. And tonight, I plan on picking up a few pointers. Or at least I hope I will.

GINA

Hanging up the phone, I have doubts for the first time about my caller. Victor wants me to *come* to the club tonight in more ways than are possible. He's a friend, if you can call one that I hook up with occasionally when the need strikes. We barely exchange words when we're together, but it's worked. He's worked for me when I need to scratch the itch. Because no matter what I let people think about me, I don't go around sleeping with people indiscriminately.

Now that Cassie is gone more than she's in town, I have more free time on my hands. And Ryder is a distraction I don't need. Why can't he be a douche like every other man out there? Why did Fletcher have to sweep my best friend off her feet and take her away? I hate that I'm lonely without her. I hate that I want what they have. And I hate myself for being a whiny bitch. *Get yourself together*.

It's been several months since I've hooked up with

Victor. *Yeah, since I hooked up with Ryder again. Don't forget that.* Decision made to go and hopefully remove the stain that is Ryder from my memory, I pick up my keys just as my phone rings.

"Yeah," I say, not bothering to look at the display, because only a few people call me.

"Gina."

The pause is so pregnant, I'm ready to believe I've forgotten to take my conversation birth control.

"Dad." The word sounds so alien on my tongue.

"Yeah, it's your old man. Not expecting to hear from me, huh?"

"Nope." That's an understatement. "Has the bitch died or something?"

"Gina," Dad admonishes.

"Whatever." The woman that Dad finally ended up with, after a string of women who seemed to have no end, likes things neat and orderly. To that point, while living with them in my youth, if anything of mine was out of place, she'd throw it away. If I ever had too many clothes, which was more than a week's worth, she'd toss them out. A couple of times, she'd thrown things away that belonged to Cassie with no remorse. Admittedly, at that time we'd lived in a house so small, my room was barely the size of my current closet, which isn't big either. But still, I'd learned to hide and hoard things for fear I wouldn't have anything one day.

"No, Marilyn is fine."

"Too bad for that." The bitch hated me and told me

on many occasions how I was a waste of space or that my dad cared for her more than me. The latter is still true.

"Look, Gina. Let's not fight, okay. I called because someone wants to meet you."

"Who?" I haven't the faintest idea. Is the bitch pregnant? She's old but not too old to have a kid. Or maybe one of Dad's other flings from the past had his kid. Not impossible.

"Your mother."

The phone suddenly feels slippery in my hands. That isn't the worst of it. I lean on the wall to find purchase so I don't crash to my knees. "What? How?"

"I guess I can come clean now. When your mom left you, there was a bunch of legal documents I had to sign along with my parents. Part of the agreement to get the money—"

"Money?" Anger almost blinds me.

"Money to take care of you. Anyway, we weren't allowed to tell you who she was more than her first name. Now she wants to meet you."

The only words I have are, "Fuck her. She's too late for all that. I have to go, *Dad*." I say the last like a curse, then hang up the phone and realize I have the shakes. What the fuck just happened?

Immediately, I dial Cassie's phone.

"Gina." The voice doesn't belong to my best friend.

"Fletcher."

He chuckles before he says, "She'll have to call you

46

back."

"I need to—"

"Her mouth is a bit occupied."

Disgusted, more with myself, I hang up, because who am I to stop him from getting his happy ending. And what does it matter anyway? There is no way I'm going to meet the woman whose DNA shares space with my dad. And money? There's no need to ponder how much she and her family paid my grandparents and dad to take me off her hands. That money would be long gone by now.

Slipping my phone into my pocket, I head down the back stairs to my Harley. I straddle the bike like I plan to straddle Victor. I will let him ride me until I can forget that phone call, forget Ryder.

The sound my Hog makes on the open road calms my soul. By the time I park it and walk into the club, I feel more in control.

"Hey," I say to the bouncer at the door.

He waves me inside, and I take the club in while peeling off my leather jacket. There's a chill in the air with fall's arrival, plus the jacket is always welcome while riding my bike. I hand it to the checker along with my phone and house rules.

I'm searching for Victor's face when he finds me first.

"Hey." His voice is like velvet, and in the past had me instantly wet.

As I stare into the golden god's eyes, sadly, my body

shows no signs of a response tonight. A certain brown-haired baseball player keeps popping in my head.

"I've missed you. I'm surprised you came, seeing that you've turned me down several times over the past few months. Are you trying the straight game?"

By straight, he means have I decided to get into a relationship.

"You know I'm not the type."

He snakes a hand around my waist and starts to pull me close. His lips are a mere inch away when my name rings out.

"Gina."

That voice is way too familiar, and I have to wonder for a second if I'm daydreaming. Over my shoulder, I get a view of my sex on a stick baseball player. Stepping out of Victor's hold, I turn to face Ryder. He stands with a giant of a man I don't recognize.

"What are you doing here?" I ask and hope people don't think there's a problem.

"Is there a problem?" Victor asks as if reading my thoughts.

"No, give me a minute, okay?" I say over my shoulder, unable to completely take my eyes off the man before me. He looks damn good, but then he always does. He wears a black T-shirt that shows off his sexy tats and pants that are tight enough to show a hint of the bulge that hides behind there.

Careful steps carry me in front of him. The friend he'd brought along seems amused. I ignore him.

"This isn't a game, Ryder."

Leaning down because he's taller than me, but not by a mile in the heels I'm wearing, he says, "I'm not playing any games. I had no idea you'd be here tonight. I came to see what this was all about."

"Okay, you've seen. You can go now. The show is over, for you anyway."

His eyes sweep down to the black corset I wear. When he meets my eyes again, I feel exposed, like I should cover myself. I don't want the vulnerability that consumes me.

"I've seen. And damn, Gina, I can't take my fucking eyes off you."

"Well, you're going to have to."

"Why?"

"Because you're leaving. This isn't your scene, and don't pretend otherwise."

Unfortunately for me, he doesn't back down. "Maybe if you let me try…"

"See, that's the thing. You've already made assumptions about me and haven't even asked."

"Look at the assumptions you've made because maybe I don't want to fuck you in plain sight. I'm not sure—"

I cut him off, "Of course you're not. I'm not an exhibitionist, Ryder. Not everyone here wants to be watched. Some want to do the watching. And this is why we will never work. I come here because I fit in. People here don't judge me for how or why I enjoy sex, like you

49

have in the last twenty seconds."

His expression, the way his eyes heat, and the half-grin that curves his sexy mouth tell me his ego wants to cheer, but he's smart enough not to say anything. I guess he knows I'm right in that he did make assumptions about me.

"I think it's time for you to leave. Besides, I have a partner for the night."

His eyes instantly grow cold, and he looks over my shoulder. "And what does he have that I don't?"

"He knows exactly what I need."

He backs up as if I took a swing at him. He narrows his gaze on me. "Really, because if I remember correctly, I got you off more than once each time we were together. Seems to me, you want—"

"A boyfriend. Absolutely not."

"Have you never had one? Not that I'm offering. Just curious."

Wanting to end this standoff, I close the distance between us. "As a matter of fact, I have. You've met him. Mark."

His eyes widen. I'm surprised he didn't know. Then again, what reason would that information have to come up in conversation until now?

"Yes, and he and I parted as friends, as I hope we can, too."

His mouth opens slightly, and because I want to slip my tongue in there, I turn away. Taking ahold of Victor's hand, I lead him out of the club, stopping only to get my phone and jacket.

"Is he the reason you haven't been around to play in a while?" Victor asks when we reach my bike.

"Does it matter?" I toss back.

He half-turns, and I see Ryder walking out. He picks up something from the ground before Victor captures my attention again.

"A piece of advice?"

Not really. "Go for it."

"This lifestyle can't last forever. If you find someone you jell with, you should give it a shot. Eventually, I'll find that partner I can't live without."

"Not sure if I should be insulted by that," I snark.

Chuckling, he says, "You know we have fun. But neither of us has ever really bothered to get to know one another. That says a lot."

He's right. "Look, I think I'm going home."

Brow raised, he asks, "Alone?"

"Yeah, I'm just not in the mood anymore."

He leans in and speaks so close to my lips, I think he's going to kiss me.

"Even if you aren't the one for me, he's a lucky guy. Make him work for it."

Straightening to his full height, he winks at me. When he walks toward his car, he calls back, "Make sure to be ready."

Ten paces away, I see the wild fury that rages in Ryder's eyes. I slip on my helmet and gun my engine out of the parking lot. I don't quite understand the possessiveness I saw in him. We barely know each other. Dark desires rage in me, though. The idea he might go back into the club and find someone else to spend his evening with has me pushing the speeding limits.

About an hour later at home, I'm scraping the bottom of a Cookies 'n Cream pint of ice cream because I was out of Double Chocolate Fudge, when a knock comes at my door.

Maybe Sam, my boss of the Dirty Hammer downstairs, needs me to fill in for someone. I'd turned my ringer off when I got to the club and hadn't turned it back on.

It's my mistake for not checking the peephole, which is a bad thing as a single woman living alone.

"Is he still here?" Ryder says, checking over my shoulder for guests.

"That's none of your business. I feel like I'm repeating myself, but why are you here, Cowboy?"

"Cowboy?"

"Yeah, you clearly think this is the OK Corral, and you've come to mark your territory. How did you know where I lived?"

When he'd shown up in my bar that time so long ago, I didn't bring him back here. I don't bring guys I don't know back to my place, ever. So he'd sprung for a hotel room that we'd made good use of.

"I'm not here to mark my territory. Sam told me."

I'm surprised. Sam is more protective of me than my own father. For him to tell some random guy where I

FASTBALL

lived knowing I'm vulnerable up here alone… well, Sam and I would have a talk. Ryder is still talking. "You dropped this." He holds up my phone. "I like the sparkle."

Needing to get away from him fast earlier, I'd pushed my phone into my pocket, or so I thought I had. I snatch the thing from his grasp. The bling on the phone had been an inside joke, and I hadn't changed the case as it gave me a little laugh every time I saw it.

"Thank you," I say sweetly. "You can leave now." He moves past me, causing me to sigh heavily. "So, what, are you going to take that big dick of yours out and piss on my floor so no other man will come over?"

He turns and nearly trips over some knickknack of mine I can't get rid of.

"Jesus, Gina, it's like a jungle in here. What's with all the stuff?"

Waving a finger at him, I say, "I wouldn't comment any further. This is my place, and two more strikes and you're out of here. You can understand that language, can't you?"

His mouth opens then closes. "Fine, but you were talking about my big dick." A smirk sprouts on his face like alfalfa. "Dressed like that, I have to assume you told the other guy to fuck off."

I glance down at my tank top and flannel shorts.

"What? You don't like the Minions. That's a hard limit for me."

Stalking toward me, he steps on something that

53

squeaks, and it makes me wince. "I want what's beneath." His hand slips easily past the waistband of my sleep shorts. He cups my sex, and I hiss. I know it's fruitless to deny the pull toward him.

"I don't want vanilla tonight," I declare.

"What do you want?"

I glance over at the doorframe that leads to my bedroom. On either side at the top of the frame are two hooks. He turns back to me, and I see wariness in his expression.

"You or me?" he asks.

"You." He nods. "Get naked, Cowboy."

As he begins, I go and get the rope made for this kind of play. It's softer and meant not to abrade the skin.

When I turn back, he stands tall, his cock long, thick, and hard. I salivate and point for him to stretch his arms up. With a stepstool, I tie his arms to either side of the frame. He faces inside my room because I have more planned for him. But first, as he looks all vulnerable, I decide to give him something for his willingness to give up control.

I take him in my mouth. Immediately, he pulls at the ropes. They aren't tied to keep him there permanently. He can get out with a little work. Sucking him to the back of my throat, I hollow my checks and work him hard. His curses spur me on. I use my hand to cradle his balls, then slide my fingers back to stroke the sensitive skin.

"Fuck, Gina, I need to touch you."

With a pop, I free him from my mouth. "That's the

point. I stand and grab the stool I left to the side. I walk into my room and get something, leaving him there to wonder. When I come back, I hook the swing on the other side where hooks are embedded on the inside of the door to my bedroom. I clamp the thing to the frame and roll on the condom over his length I grabbed on the way. Then I use the stool to get in the chair.

"What the fuck?"

Damn, if he isn't the perfect height. No adjustments needed, I grab his dick and pull myself closer. I've never tried this before, but as he sinks inside me, he starts to buck. I clasp my hands on either side of his face and kiss him. I don't want the swing to bang into him, so I wrap my legs around him. This keeps us on track as he pushes inside me with delicious friction.

Siding my hand down, I tweak his nipples.

"Gina, you're going to make me come. Grip the base of my dick if you don't want me to."

Instead, I pull back so he can see himself slide in and out of me to a point, and I start to rub circles over my clit.

"Fuck," he growls. I feel him pulse inside of me.

I can't help but wonder what it would feel like if he wasn't encased in rubber.

It's only a few more bounces with his face lost in pleasure, before he says, "Let me loose, so I can take care of you."

RYDER

ot fucking damn. Gina has all kinds of tricks up her sleeves, and after this, I'm a willing student. If this is what she means by left of vanilla, I'm ready to go all Chunky Monkey and Phish Food without a doubt.

"Untie me, Gina."

"Hang on, Cowboy." She loosens the rope around me and says, "You know these weren't tight. You could've wiggled your way out if you wanted."

"But that's not the point, right?"

She sends me a sly smile. "Now you're getting it."

"Good. My turn. Get back in that swing. I need some dessert."

The swing comes equipped with stirrups, and I intend to make great use of them. Placing a heel in each one, I spread her wide, but I have to bend at an awkward angle due to my height. Then I see the adjustment cable so I raise it up, stopping when it gets to the perfect level.

"Fuck, I feel like I'm at the ceiling," she jokes.

"Hush. It's my turn, remember?"

She doesn't know it, but I have a few tricks up my sleeve and I intend to employ them tonight. She's spread before me, and I use my fingers to open her up to me, like the petals of a flower. My finger easily slides in so I add another, making sure to press on her G-spot. Then my tongue runs up and down, rimming her opening around my fingers as they work her. She's squirming, trying to get me to lick her clit, but I'm teasing her a bit longer.

When she's practically grinding herself against me, I press my tongue on her and focus entirely on that tiny bud. Dropping my mouth over it, I suck and flick, until she's thrashing around. My thumb is unoccupied, so I decide to put it into action. Using some of her own wetness, I slide it around her and then rub it over her tight little bud in the back.

"Ryder, Ryder, Ryder," she keeps repeating my name as her orgasm plows into her. Listening to her husky voice gets me hard as fuck. It's time to lower the swing again. Afterward, I roll on another condom, leaving my thumb to play around her ass. Then I spread her wide and plunge into her, fucking her hard, exactly the way she loves it.

"Play with your tits, Gina."

There's no asking her twice. She's on it like crazy, teasing and pinching her nipples. Shit, it's sexy as hell.

My balls slam into her with every thrust, and she lifts her head to watch.

"Damn, I'm gonna come. Are you close?" I ask. Her head shakes like a bobble-headed doll. "Use your hand."

She massages a circle on her clit and bites her lower lip. Her black curls are a tangled mess, and all I can think of is kissing her until her lips are swollen and her face is chafed from my scruff.

When her climax hits, I feel her inner muscles tighten in rhythm against my dick and squeeze it, milking my cum out of me.

"Fuck, you're tight."

When I'm finally dry, I say, "Bathroom?"

An arm lifts and points me in the right direction. This place looks like a nuclear bomb went off. Not that it's dirty. The sink is spotless, and the rest of it is clean, but there is shit every-fucking-where. When I come back out, Gina is still situated in the swing. I unhook her ankles, pick her up and carry her to the bed, laying her down gently. I crawl in behind her.

But I'm not done with her yet. Now on to the kissing part. But when I try, she puts a hand on my chest and makes a weak attempt to shove me away.

"What? I can fuck you, but I can't kiss you?"

"Something like that."

"Not in my world." My mouth crashes onto hers as my hand tunnels into her mane. I tilt her head so our lips align perfectly, and then I explore every secret her mouth can possibly hold. Knowing Gina is my goal, I want

FASTBALL

to discover everything there is to find. She's made me more curious than any other woman I've ever met.

I kiss her cheek, ear, neck—oh, do I kiss her neck. She writhes, then moans and I've hit a target here.

"You like this? Tell me what you want. Do you want me to fuck you again? Do you want me to eat your pussy? You have an amazing pussy, Gina. Do you want me to play your kinky games? You want to tie me up? Flog me? What is it? Tell me," I say against her nipple I started sucking. She arches her back, bringing me closer to my goal. Her skin is smooth like silk, and she tastes perfect, just the right amount of sweet mixed with salt.

"Blindfold me," she says. "It heightens the senses. And I'm game for anything, including anal beads as long as you know what you're doing. I have lots of other toys, too."

"Where's your toy box, my wild thing?"

She points to her closet, but it's a little scary looking in there, almost like an obstacle course. "On the shelf. Use whatever you want. Just surprise me. The lube's in the box, too."

With apprehension, I enter her closet and look for said box. She calls out from the bed, "It's a pink suitcase looking thing."

Christ. How many toys does she have? I find the suitcase, and the damn thing weighs a ton. Opening it up, I find a blindfold and put it on her. Then I go back and look at everything in the box, and honestly, I'm not sure what some of the things are.

59

"Uh, Gina, I don't know what some of these are."

"Most of them are Lelos."

"What's a Lelo?"

"It's a vibrator brand, and they just look a little weird."

"Oh." Who knew? I thought a vibrator was a vibrator. But then there's a flogger, some long feathers, some fur-lined handcuffs, long tethers with cuffs attached, and some other gadgets. And lots of lube. Warming lube, ice lube, flavored lube, and body paints. I grab some warming lube, the tethers, a feather, and a couple of the funky looking vibrators. Let's see where this takes us.

Gina lies there waiting, so I attach each ankle and wrist to the cuffs and then tether her to the bedposts. "Now you're my prisoner." I chuckle.

As I step away, the absolute pleasure of the vision that lies before me pummels me from the inside with a sensation I can't quite describe. From the glorious tumble of tangled locks, to her breasts that fit my mouth to perfection, down to the curves that make my mouth water, I'm reduced to a single mass of need I haven't felt since ... well, I've never felt before. And to be honest, I can have any woman I want. They're easy to come by. Ever since high school, they've all but thrown themselves at me, even when I didn't want them. It's only gotten worse since I've entered the pros. But none of them have interested me like this—ever since this dark-haired crazy ass bartender with a fortress constructed around her so damn thick I doubt I'll ever tear down walked into my life. But maybe, just maybe, now's my chance to start chipping away at the thing.

She licks her lips, and it makes me want to sink my teeth into them. Instead, I bend her knees, putting her feet flat on the bed and spreading her legs. Then I tighten the tethers so she can't move.

"Is this comfortable?"

"Yeah."

"Good." Admittedly, I'm a bit nervous, which is an alien feeling for me. Usually I have no qualms when it comes to things involving bedroom activities, but this is a new venture for me. Pushing all inhibitions aside, I grab ahold of the lube and squeeze until the right amount is on my hand. Then I rub it on her sex, inside and out until she wriggles beneath my ministrations, which I should add are thorough. Next on my list is to use one of her fancy vibrators. I want to see exactly why she has so many of these. I grab the purple one that is soft, with two actual appendages—one large and one small. I check it out for a second, trying to decide what kind of play I'm going to do.

"What are you doing? Baking a cake?" her smart mouth asks.

Not bothering to answer, I run the feather from her chin, down her neck, and stop right above her sex. She moans. "Does this feel like a cake to you?" I whisper next to her ear.

"No. No cake."

She licks her lips, and it's with great difficulty I don't fuck that sassy mouth of hers. Only I keep teasing her with the feather instead. Her nipples are stone hard, like diamond peaks as they rise to the feather's touch, and that's when I turn on the vibrator. I'm surprised by how silent it is. I don't know, for some reason I expected something more powerful. But when I slide it over her sex, she cries out, begging for more.

"Tell me how much more you want, Gina? All of it? Or just a little?"

"All." Her chest heaves with her reply, and my dick grows harder right along with it. Fuck me. I'm not sure I can take this shit.

Sliding the vibrator inside her, the other tip vibrates against her clit, and too bad they don't make the male equivalent of these things. Because from the way she's squirming and groaning, and goddamn it's hot as hell, this must be fucking nirvana. And I just learn something—this is more arousing than I can take. Her wrists and ankles jerk wildly against the restraints as she comes, but the way she breathes out my name is the most erotic thing ever. Except I really want my mouth where that piece of equipment is. So I do exactly that. I've never gone down on a lubed up woman before, but I'm open to it. And when I do—surprise. It's strawberry flavored.

After I lick and suck her to another orgasm, she tells me to let her loose. But I only agree after I kiss that smart mouth of hers. Once I get my fill, I untether her, and she pushes me down, and straddles me. Then she proceeds to fuck me like I've never been fucked before. The other times we've been together were nothing compared to this. She bites, scratches, and every time I get close, she stops, either sliding off me altogether, or sitting still until the urge to come passes. My nipples will never be the same after tonight. But the crème de la crème is when she has me bend my knees as she's on top, and right as I'm getting close again, she sticks her finger up my ass and I come like the goddamn space shuttle taking off. I swear to God my eyes roll back in my head and I almost lose consciousness. Her voice finally comes to me from a distance.

"Ryder? Hey, you here?"

"Um, yeah. I'm here. Where'd you think I was?"

"I don't know. I was talking to you, and you weren't answering."

"Oh. I was in recovery." Swallowing the lump of whatever has formed in my throat, I blink and look at this … this unbelievable woman in bed with me. "Who are you?"

"Gina."

"Come and give me a kiss, *Gina*, because I'm too weak to move."

"Well, I'll let you rest a little, but I'm not even close to being done with you yet, *Ryder*."

I have a feeling this is going to be a long, but unforgettable night. I only hope I can show up at practice on Monday morning.

GINA

When is the last time I've ever felt this well fucked? I can't remember if ever. The throbbing between my legs is a constant reminder like a blinking sign that reads *Ryder's been here*.

"Gina."

I turn to find my boss, Sam, frowning at me. He must have been asking me a question or something the way his suspicion grows.

"What?" I say jovially.

His eyes narrow. "You're smiling. What, did you win the lottery or something?"

"Or something."

"Maybe that something has a name."

Which reminds me that I need to rip Sam a new one. "How could you tell some guy where I live?"

"You mean, Ryder Wilde, Fletcher's cousin, the Fletcher that's married to your best friend, Cassidy. I

64

thought he was safe. And besides, by the grin you are sporting, things turned out good."

Unable to wipe the smile from my face, I focus on the bar and continue to wipe it down, ignoring his supposition. The lunch crowed has breezed through, and as soon as the last customer leaves, I'm free to head upstairs before the dinner rush.

Eleven minutes and thirty seconds pass before the guy finally pays and leaves me shit for tip, but who's counting? Normally, I'll cuss and threaten Sam to quit for the millionth time. But today I find myself skipping up the back steps as if Pharrell's song "Happy" plays in the background.

Only when I get my head out of the clouds do I realize a woman stands at my door. Instantly, my good mood fades. She doesn't look that old, but still I'm cautious.

"Gina Ferraro?"

"Who's asking?"

She holds out a hand I only glance at. Her smile falters, and a business-like expression covers her face. She drops her hand. "My name is Sara. Ryder Wilde sent me. I'm an organizer."

I'm going to kill him.

"Oh, did he?"

She isn't fooled by my wide grin. There must be murder in my eyes. I push past her and let myself in the door because I'm not going to have this conversation out in the open.

"Wow, he's right."

Spinning around, I say, "Right about what?"

Her professional demeanor is back, and I can see why Ryder knows her. She's beautiful in that polished way I'll never be. An ugly part of me wonders if he's banged her.

"He said you had a lot of…" She searches for a word. "… collectables and things that might look better displayed and organized."

Not bothering to comment, I pull out my phone and dial the asshat in question.

"Gina."

Giving the woman my back, I say, "Don't *Gina* me."

"You've met her," he deadpans. "And don't snarl at me. I just thought I could do something nice for you."

"Nice is flowers, not a decorator."

"I'm not a decorator," Sara chimes, because I hadn't exactly gotten out of earshot.

"Send her away if you want, but I've already paid her."

Grrrr. How could he possibly know that would be the magic answer? There is no way I want him wasting money on me.

"Fine," I growl.

"You should know I got shit today because of you."

That makes me smile. And I walk toward my bedroom to give us some privacy. I don't say anything to Sara because I doubt she's going to leave.

Once I close the door, I say, "Why is that?"

66

"Because I think I pulled a muscle in my ass."

A bubble of laughter bursts out of me. "Like my finger there, huh?"

"Don't remind me. That shit isn't natural."

"Puns upon puns," I say. "But it made you come for days."

"It sure did. But I'll be damn if I tell Fletcher about it."

"Don't you worry. I've schooled Cassie on it. I'm sure Fletcher's gotten the full treatment."

We trade laughter for a few seconds, and damn, if it doesn't feel good to be happy for once in my life.

"As much as I want to sit here on the phone with you talking dirty shit, I have to go. I won't get to see your pretty ass for a few days. But you know that, don't you?"

"Why would you think I would know your game schedule?"

"The calendar on your refrigerator was my first clue."

Damn, he'd seen that.

"It was a free magnet I got in the mail from a realtor."

"Uh huh. Do you own some property I don't know about?"

Crap, I'm striking out seriously.

"Don't you worry about that, Cowboy. Now, go pitch a no-hitter."

"Not sure that is possible. My arm feels like a wet noodle."

"I bet your dick feels the same," I counter.

"Actually, my dick perked up as soon as I heard that voice of yours."

"You're such a flirt. How many times have you used these lines?"

"Never," he breathes. "And how about another line that makes total sense?"

"What's that?"

"Dream about me, Gina."

Rolling my eyes, I say, "You wish. Your cheesy lines aren't getting you anywhere. Besides, we're just friends. And who knows how many friends I can make while you're out of town."

I hang up as he tries to say something. Laughing to myself, I go to talk to Sara.

"Fine. Do your worst. But if you throw anything away, I'll personally clutter the room with your face."

Her jaw drops, but I walk out the door not wanting to watch. Personally, I like my chaotic mess. It makes me feel in control of my own destiny. But I couldn't explain that to Ryder. Best to limit our conversations to naughty talk only. Whatever this is we have together won't last. He'll get bored and move on. I need to protect myself. However, there isn't any harm in enjoying him while he's interested. Or is there? And when in the hell did I let a guy rule the show? *This time, Gina.*

Later that night, I'm working the bar. It's full of Cougars fans. Ryder's game is on, and I'm trying not to keep my eyes glued to the screen. From what I've heard with groans from the crowd, he's playing like shit for most of this inning. And they are going to pull him if he loads up the bases with his next pitch.

"Come on, baby."

After the words slip off my tongue, I actually stick it out and glare at it.

"I can give you a place to put that."

I glance up to see a sexy tourist sitting at the bar studying me. I've never seen him in town, so I know he's not local. I may not know everyone, but I've seen everyone at least once in the twenty plus years I've lived here.

He has a faint accent and dark entrancing eyes. He's the kind of once in a lifetime stranger I might have hooked up with in the past. Hadn't Ryder been that? He'd been my annual itch of fun. That *screw it fuck* I do sparingly because once in a while a woman needs to be reckless. But my quota is currently filled.

"And where would that be?" The glacial stare I give him should make his balls shrivel.

"Ah, feisty. I like that."

Damn, if his accent isn't sexy on his tongue. It makes you want to do the Italian rumba or some kind of dance. But who cares, he looks every bit the Italian stallion. And something tells me by the way he hasn't backed down, he can back up his flirtation.

But then the place gets quiet, and I glance up at the TV screen. The manager on the field has just left the mound. How could I have forgotten Ryder? The camera zooms in on him, and his face is a mask of concentration.

"Come on, baby," I say again, without admonishing myself.

When he lets the ball fly, I barely see it. I let out a breath when the catcher reveals the ball in his glove.

The bar is still so quiet because apparently the game is on the line.

The camera comes back to my guy. He spits out something I don't care to think of until the camera pans in closer still. His mouth is sin, and I have the sudden urge to want to ride it. The angle switches, and we see the manager doing some complicated rain dance to signal what pitch he wants Ryder to throw next. The screen switches back to Ryder, and he nods. He winds up and lets the ball fly. I swear I need my eyes checked because it isn't until the instant replay on slow-mo do I see the fastball he threw.

"One more, baby," I mumble.

I'm not even aware I'm saying it until the stranger repeats the last word. Ignoring him, I don't take my eyes off the screen. I wait like everyone else.

The pitch leaves Ryder's hand like he's a magician. The ball is just there in the catcher's glove a second before players swarm the field like ants to the mound, swallowing Ryder until I can't see him anyone. Apparently, it's a big deal. Normally, they don't let the starters pitch an entire game. But he'd had a no-hitter until that last inning. Somehow he convinced the manager to let him stay in. This will up his ranking for sure.

"So, you have a boyfriend, yes?"

I glance back at the stranger and wonder why I thought him so attractive. Okay, maybe he is. But honestly, it takes one move of my legs to remember all the reasons why I don't need a one-night stand. Still, the stranger doesn't have it quite right.

"Why would you say that?"

His eyes cast to the right where a delivery guy stands with a vase full of peach colored roses.

"Is there a Gina Ferraro here?"

"That's me," I answer begrudgingly. Now the stranger knows my name.

"I have a delivery here for you."

I bite back the *duh* that wants to lash out of my mouth. Signing at the bottom where indicated, I shift my focus to the gorgeous flowers for a long minute. No one has ever sent me flowers before, not even Mark. But then we dated when we were young and jobless. I've had guys give me grocery store bundles in offer to get in my pants. I'd turned each one of them down along with their sorry flowers. But I've never gotten a thought out delivery before.

The card reads simply.

Just because ~ Ryder

I feel pinpricks of tears in the back of my eyes. Fuck that. I blink that shit away. Just because no guy had ever done something so nice didn't mean I had to get mushy about it.

"Since you don't have a boyfriend, will you let me take you out to dinner?"

My eyes leave the roses in favor of the stranger. "It's past dinner, and if you haven't guessed, I'm working."

Could he be that dense?

"I didn't mean tonight. Tomorrow or whenever you have a free moment."

Sexy as he is, I'm not in the mood. I want to go to the back and call my baseball player and tell him what a jerk he is for almost making me cry.

I say, "I'll be free in like..." I tap my chin and add, "never."

My stranger doesn't give up. He reaches into his pocket and pulls out a card. "That's too bad. I find you rather attractive. And something tells me we would have a lot of fun together." His eyes caress me, and I barely manage not to shiver. It isn't like I want the man, but he oozes sex. It's just I'm not in the market right now.

As I start to slide the card back toward him, he places his warm palm on the back of my hand.

"You'll want that. You remind me so much of your mother."

I snatch my hand away as if I was burned.

Cue in the heavy sigh he lets out. "You're spitting images of each other. Though I must say, you're far more my type."

"You can leave now," I order.

"Yes, she thought you might respond that way."

Out of thin air he produces an envelope and sends it

across the bar top to me. "Read this and then give me a call. I have a feeling we'll be having dinner anyway."

He winks, fucking winks at me. I watch him walk out in tailored pants and an expensive shirt. When I glance down at his card, I see he's a lawyer. That only makes me curious about what's inside the letter. I stuff it into my back pocket before getting back to work. I want to be happy about the gorgeous flowers Ryder sent. Instead, the envelope weighs on me.

I glance up in time to watch Ryder leaving the field when a zealous fan jumps down. The next thing I know her lips are on his. Before she can be hauled away, the mic zooms in as she lifts her shirt. Her blurred tits are on display as she begs Ryder to sign them.

Disgusted, I turn away to fill a drink order.

Why in the world would I ever think I could compete when women offer themselves to him all the time? Didn't Riley say that her brother was a lover of many women?

When I finally make it upstairs to my apartment, dog tired, it feels like Ikea had a blue light special that ended up in my apartment.

Bookcases flank either side of my TV with all my trinkets and knickknacks. Everything is in a place that makes fucking sense, if I have to admit it. But the tears don't come until I get in my room. All the clothes that had been in organized piles on the floor are gone. Panicked, I throw open the closet doors, afraid that *the bitch, my stepmonster* had somehow gotten in my apartment and threw away all my clothes. But there they are, all in color-coordinated fashion. The closet had a makeover, too, and I have shelves for sweaters and shoes. Everything somehow fits.

My phone rings off in the distance, but I can't. I fall to my knees and cry like I haven't done since I was a teenager. Everything is so pristine, yet it feels like I've lost all control over my life. The organization, my mom wanting to show up in my life, Ryder, and most important, how I can't have him. And no matter how irrational it is, I can't stop crying.

RYDER

ina's not answering her phone, which is weird. I called Cassie to make sure everything was fine with her because I was beginning to worry, but she assures it is. After Monday night's game, I was so stoked, I needed to hear her voice, yet no answer. I figured maybe she was at work and couldn't talk, but I called two more times, well past closing when she should've been home, and still nothing. Was she with someone else? We're not committed, but what we shared over the weekend, I find it hard to believe she would want to be with another man so soon.

Tuesday morning, I wake up in a grumpy ass mood. I want to talk to my girl. Wait. What's this *my girl* shit? Slow down, junior. She won't even answer her fucking phone and I'm calling her mine. That isn't right.

When I get into the kitchen, I slam things around in my effort to get some breakfast in me. We have another game tonight and getting my head on straight is top priority. Another glance at my phone yields zip. So being the pussy ass that I am, I text her.

Hey, just checking in. I called last night, but must've missed you. Call when you can. Hope you got my—just because. ☺ *R*

There. That sounds generic enough. I hit send before I chicken out. And then I overthink things, as usual. That smiley face was over the top. And I shouldn't have mentioned the flowers. What the fuck was I thinking?

The coffee is close, so I grab the pot and pour. But, of course, it comes streaming out onto my hand and burns the shit out of me.

"Goddamn motherfuckingsonofabitch." I turn on the cold water and put my hand under it.

"Will you stop making all this racket? I didn't get in until six and have only slept a couple of hours." My sister emerges from her room upstairs and stomps into the kitchen full of fire.

"Hmph."

"Is that your explanation? Hmph? What crawled up your ass and died?" I'd like to say *Gina's finger*, but I keep my mouth shut. "Well?"

Taking my chances, I look up at her and almost laugh. Her eyes are smeared with mascara, her hair looks like a live critter has taken up residence there, and she's wearing a robe with Snoopy and Charlie Brown all over it.

"Jesus, you look like shit."

"Fuck you, Ryder. I've been playing in a tournament

all week, which by the way, I came in third. Fuck you very much. And thanks for the supportive phone calls and texts."

Oh, God, I'm the biggest douche of a brother.

"Oh, Ri, that's fabulous. I really mean it. And I'm sorry. I was bu—"

"Busy, I know. You're always busy, Ryder." Then she pokes her index finger into my chest. And there's one thing about golfers. They have strong hands. "Let me tell you something, buster. You're not the only one in the universe with a busy life."

"Right. Gotcha. Pro golfers are busy, too."

"Damn straight we are. I spend all day on the course, playing a minimum of thirty-six holes, and that doesn't count the driving range or the putting green. I also work out in the gym every day, so stick that in your pipe and smoke it."

"I don't smoke. Remember?" As soon as I say the words, I regret them. She's not in the mood for banter. Riley has this thing about me not respecting her sport, but she's dead wrong. I am in awe of my sister. Out of the two of us, she is hands down the better athlete, and had she been born a male, I hate to say it, but she would've kicked my ass in every sport I played, including baseball. Her hand-eye coordination is brilliant, and her accuracy is dead-on. She can nail a ball, and I'm not just talking with a golf club. Put a bat, tennis racket, Ping-Pong paddle, just about anything in her hands, and she kills her opponent. And competitive—her picture should be next to the word in Merriam-Webster's.

"It was a weak joke, Riley. You know I think you're the best, but I don't tell you enough. I'm sorry. And congratulations." I pull her in my arms and give her a hug. "Nice robe, by the way."

"Shut up, Ryder." Her crooked grin tells me her anger has dissipated.

"Sorry my foul temper woke you up. I didn't know you took the red-eye. And I didn't think I was that loud."

"Last minute thing. And, yeah, I could've heard you the next block over. Why are you such a grouch this morning?"

I shrug, not wanting to get into the Gina discussion.

"Come on. Tell your big sissy."

I have to laugh at her when she says that. Older by two minutes, she's my big sister all right. "It's nothing."

"Clearly, it is. You won last night in an amazing finale, and here you are, the morning after, acting like you gave the game away."

There has to be a way to get her off this topic, so I examine my hand, pretending it hurts, even though it's fine.

She doesn't buy it. Grabbing my hand, she says, "Hey, I'm here. Talk to me."

"Okay. Fine. It's Gina."

"Gina? What happened? Did you do something?"

"Yeah, I sent her flowers, and now I haven't heard from her."

"When did you send them?"

"Yesterday."

She busts out laughing. "Oh my God. It's been a day, dude. Calm your testicles down."

"And this is why I didn't want to tell you."

"Damn, you're serious, yeah?"

Since I am, I don't answer.

"So tell me everything."

Like hell. There is no way that shit will pass through my lips. "Not much to say. I saw her last weekend. We had fun. I sent flowers."

"And you're this trippy over her. Huh-uh. There's more to it, Ryder Wilde."

"And if there is, it's none of your business, Riley. You may be my sister, but that doesn't entitle you to everything in my personal life."

"Well, I'll be. You like her. More than you usually like a woman."

"Again, my business."

"Just remember, bro, she's my friend, too, so don't put me in the middle of anything."

"Wouldn't dream of it."

"My advice, send her a spa gift certificate. There's not a woman alive who wouldn't love one of those."

A spa gift certificate. If I were a betting man, I'd wager Gina has never received one of those from any of her previous boyfriends … no, that's not exactly right. She claims not to have those. Or whatever she would refer to them as.

"Nice idea, sis. I think I'll do that."

"Asheville. The Grove Park Inn Spa. Very chic. Fletcher's mom always goes on and on about it."

"Thanks." I hug her and go do the order up. There are all sorts of things, but I go all out and get her the day package. She will be pampered like she's never been—or that's my hope anyway.

The rest of the day is consumed with me obsessively checking my phone like a girl to see if I got a text from Gina and then heading to the stadium to prepare for the game.

The team is jacked up with adrenaline when I walk in. Cheers nearly crack my eardrum, but it's an awesome feeling. One thing I'll never do is take credit for a win, so I shout out, "You guys did an unbelievable job last night!"

Guys bang the inside of lockers with fists and kick their feet against them, too. The noise level is stupid crazy.

"Are we gonna do a repeat tonight?" I yell.

That question brings down the house. Coach Martin walks in with Ms. Whitestone, the owner of the team, and they both congratulate the team on our bang up job last night. Then Ms. Whitestone goes on to give us her little talk. She comes in once a week or so, and a lot of the guys ogle her. They all talk about what a MILF she is. She is an attractive older woman, maybe mid-forties, with black hair, but I'm into women my own age.

After she leaves, the rest of the players dress for the game. I head to the trainers' office to get therapy on my arm because it's dead after last night. Gina enters my thoughts, but I shove her out because I need to be laser-focused right now.

Down the hall, I run into my pitching coach.

"Are you going to be ready in a few days, Wilde? They're gonna be wanting revenge after those final pitches you threw last night."

"Got it covered, Coach."

He pats me on the back, saying, "I know you do. Just making sure. Old lady Whitestone is anxious."

"Aren't we all being this close to the playoffs? I don't need reminding."

After therapy, I watch the start of the game from the monitor in the dugout. The first four innings are in the bag for us. Four no-hitters and we're up three zip. But then there's a turn around. As the pitcher throws the ball, his grip eases too soon, and the ball doesn't do exactly as he'd planned. The batter takes a swing and ends up with a double. The tough thing is, it happens again, and this time they score with a slide into home plate on an error in the outfield. Fuck. He strikes the next batter out, and they head to the dugout.

"What the hell was that?" our pitching coach asks him when they get in the dugout.

"Ball got loose."

"Twice? In a row?"

Our manager gives Coach a scathing look. Coach just shakes his head, and he catches my eye. I know he wishes my arm were rested. And so do I. I'd love nothing more than to get in the game. But now my hand stings, so I shake it out.

"What's going on there?" he asks, grabbing my hand. "What happened?"

"Burnt it on some coffee, is all."

"Jesus Christ, Wilde, why the hell didn't you say something earlier?"

"It really doesn't hurt. I'm fine."

"Like hell. We can't afford you having any injuries."

He calls for one of the trainers. They examine it and recommend a wrap.

"How the hell can I pitch with it wrapped? I won't be able to feel my grip on the ball."

Coach gives me one of his *are you shitting me* looks. "You're on rest days now anyway, so what difference does it make?"

When he puts it like that, he leaves without an argument.

"Keep it wrapped," he tells the trainer. "And put something in there to make sure it heals fast."

The trainer walks me over to the bench and puts some kind of goop on my hand. The problem is, it's located between my thumb and index finger, making it difficult to open and close my hand. I should've taken better care of it after it happened and not let myself get so distracted by buying shit for Gina. The spa thing and then I went to that Lelo website and bought some couple's vibrator I thought might send her a message.

"How's that? I tried to keep it so your thumb and

fingers are free, leaving you your dexterity."

I flex my fingers and hand, and it doesn't feel bad. "Hey, Coach, toss me a ball," I yell. One comes flying and the trainer has to duck.

"Asshole," he says.

"Yeah, he can't throw worth a shit," I say. I grab the ball, toss it in the air a bit, and add, "I think this might be okay."

The coach says, "You have a couple of days off to rest that arm and hand."

"But I wanna get in the pen and test drive this thing." I hold up my hand and wiggle it around, knowing it will set him off. I love yanking his chain. His face gets as red as a tomato.

"Sit your ass back down. You're out for the next five days. Maybe more if necessary."

"Maybe I should just take an island vacation somewhere. You know, go and drink some fruity umbrella drinks and hang out on the beach."

"I'll give you fruity umbrella drinks. Right up your ass. Listen up, Wilde. I'd rather have you playing the rest of the month than for you to tear that hand up or your arm. So off your feet and on your ass. Now."

In a characteristic coach's move imitating him, I take my hat off and throw it on the dugout floor. He finally figures out that I've been playing him.

"You're an asshole, Wilde."

Unfortunately, we end up losing the game, which is no fault of mine, so the next two are crucial. When I get home, Riley is all about my hand.

"It's that fucking coffee burn. I'm off for five days. I should be fine."

"Shit, Ryder. I didn't think it was a big deal."

"Apparently, it is. Look, I'm beat. We have a double-header tomorrow, so I need to crash. Even though I'll be benching it, it'll be a long day."

"Not even one beer?"

"Okay. One."

We shoot the breeze, and I hit the sack after our beer. In the morning, I'm afraid to look at my hand. The trainer wrapped it again after I showered and said to leave it until the morning. Now's the big reveal. I take off the bandage, and it does look a lot better. It hurts a lot less, too.

After my shower, I head to the kitchen for a huge breakfast. I need all the calories I can get. Six eggs, four pieces of toast, a protein shake, two bananas, some coffee, and two giant glasses of milk later and I'm rubbing my stomach.

"Christ, Ryder. Won't you puke with all that in you?" Riley asks.

"Huh-uh. This will hold me until the seventh inning stretch of game one, maybe. Then I have these to fill in. It's a long day." I hold up some gigantic protein bars Fletcher turned me onto because they're high in calories and do the trick.

"But damn, it's not like you're expending a lot just sitting there. Baseball is like watching paint dry."

"Maybe, but I'll have a lot of nervous energy."

"Yeah, okay. Keep eating like that and you'll have to be getting a solid workout from nine to five every day to keep from going up ten sizes."

"Whatever. I'll worry about my body, and you worry about yours, big sis."

I get ready, grab my bag, and go. Maybe Riley's right. The last thing I want is to get fat for Gina. Pushing those thoughts aside, I focus on the game and hope we pull this one out. Luckily, whatever the trainer did and sitting out yesterday had really helped. My arm feels like I could pitch, and my hand feels good. It's still wrapped, but it doesn't bother me because my fingers and thumb are free. We go on to win both games, and I end my day on a high.

That night, I call Gina again, but no answer. She had to receive at least the spa gift, and it's a little hurtful that she didn't call or text me to express her thanks. I didn't take her for that kind of girl. Since I have the next couple of nights free, I decide to chance it and go visit her.

I put a call into Fletcher to see if it's okay if I stay at his place.

"Cassie won't be there, so it's fine. My only rule is to leave it like you found it."

"No worries on that, man. Is there a key somewhere?"

"Yeah." He tells me where they have one hidden by the back porch. "And I know you're probably going to see Gina, so good luck with her. She's slippery like an eel,

Ryder."

"Tell me something I don't know. Take care."

When I get to Waynesville, it's getting dark and close to seven. I head to Fletcher and Cassie's, locate the key, and check the place out. It's nice what they've done so far in the renovations. My next stop is the Dirty Hammer, hoping Gina will be working.

As soon as I walk in, I see Sam at the bar. This isn't good.

"Hey, Ryder. You looking for Gina?"

"Yeah, she here?"

"No, she's out to dinner. I'm not sure where, but there aren't too many places in town. I'd start at the Chef's Grill and work my way down if I were you."

"Thanks, Sam. I will." And I head down the street.

It's Thursday, so not overly crowded, even though fall is hitting, when things will soon heat up in town. I walk in and scan the room. The place isn't very big at all, so in no time I find her, but there's a huge problem. She's not alone. The someone with her is male and dark-haired, and she just laughed at something he said. Then her head tilts as I watch, and that's when it happens. Our eyes connect, her face collapses, and I turn and walk away. Guess I know why she never returned my calls or texts now. This is not what I expected at all.

Retracing my steps, I head back to the Dirty Hammer. I need to get hammered in a bad way.

"Guess she wasn't there, huh?" Sam asks.

"No, she was, but she had a date. Can you give me a

shot of tequila? No, make that three."

"Sorry, man, and I got you covered."

Three shots appear before me, and I'm downing my third when a voice drifts over my shoulder. "Hey, Ryder."

GINA

Dinner with the lawyer has been an eye-opening experience. I'm not sure what to do with the information he's given me, but I've been thrown for a loop seeing Ryder walk in. When he walks out, I'm rattled, more so than the news I received.

"I have to go," I say abruptly.

"Boyfriend?" the lawyer says, who on any other day might have been my next conquest.

"No. And thanks for dinner."

I start to pull out my wallet, but he stops me. "I've got this."

The accent rolls off his tongue in ways that are sinful, but he isn't my baseball player. I leave and step outside to breathe. I've avoided all of Ryder's calls. His gifts made me feel special, and I didn't know how to handle it. He seems so genuine, but I'm a coward. The thought of heartbreak scares me more than death.

Before I make up my mind on what I'm going to do,

my dinner companion is by my side. I pretend as though I don't notice and head to the bar. I need a drink. Here's to hoping my silence sends a message that I want to be left alone.

Lost in my thoughts when I open the front door, I see Ryder, beautiful and everything a girl could want, sitting with a tumbler cradled in his hands. He's staring at it as though it has all the answers in the world.

"Hey, Ryder," I call out boldly. Bravado has been my shield. Hopefully, it will work tonight.

He turns, but that's about the time the lawyer circles his hand around my arm, turning me to face him.

"Are you sure you're okay?"

I nod. "I'll be fine. Thanks again for dinner."

His eyes are filled with desire, and I get the faintest hint he might quite possibly kiss me. I step out of his hold.

"I'll let you know what I decide," I say, then turn and walk over to Ryder.

"What's shaking, Cowboy?"

The grin on my face is supposed to get him to forgive me of any sins he might think I've committed. Only he doesn't speak to me. Instead, he drains his glass.

"What brings you to these parts?" I try again, nerves getting the best of me.

His silence makes me feel like a desperate teenage girl who drew hearts of her crush's name in the margins of her notebook. That's something I've never done.

"Oh, I don't know. I came to see why I can't get a

response from a woman I've called a number of times. I guess I have my answer."

"Ryder, it's not—"

"Save it, Gina. I don't chase after women. I don't have to. The one time I try…"

He shrugs. From his back pocket he produces some bills he lays on the bar countertop. When he stands, I fight back a wave of unwelcome feelings … fear.

"Just give me a chance to explain," I try.

His frosty eyes land on mine. "You don't owe me anything. You made it clear from the start. I was the fool for thinking…"

Trailing off again, he doesn't finish his sentence.

"Then let's not talk," I suggest.

In a risky move, I step forward, get on my toes, and plant my lips against his. His soft lips are hard and unyielding, before he finally relaxes. His arm coils around my waist, and his mouth parts. I snake my tongue inside, getting a taste of expensive whiskey tinged with tequila.

Pulling back, I let my hand slide down his arm and wrap it in his. Then I tug him forward and lead him through the private hallway for employees only. There, I find the back door. Outside again, I scurry up the steps to my apartment. Quickly, I unlock the door and yank him inside. His eyes take in the clutter-free space that still weirds me out, but I've done my best to maintain the calm and get over my issues. Although in a rebellious move known only to me, I toss my dirty clothes on the closet floor and not in the provided hamper.

He starts to speak, but I put a finger to his lips and force his back against the door. I slide to my knees and work at freeing his beautiful cock from his pants.

At half-mast, I take it in my hands and feel it grow. I lift my eyes to meet his as I open my mouth and suck him toward the back of my throat, while trying to get most of him inside without gagging.

His eyes change as if a fire burns in them. He takes his hand, threads it through my hair before pulling me forward and back to guide the pace he needs. I clamp my lips down hard, knowing men like a little more pressure.

Groaning, his cock swells and it's becoming harder to get most of him in my mouth. I relax my throat and swallow, opening myself to take him deeper.

"That's it, baby. Take it."

His voice is husky, and a growing need bursts in my core.

"Touch yourself, Gina. Show me how wet you are," he adds as if reading my thoughts.

I do as he bids and hold up two damp fingers in the way of a boy scout. A rumbling sound comes from him a second before he pulls me off. Then my wrist is in his hand as he draws me to a standing position. He sucks my fingers in his mouth and licks them clean. I have to say that shit is hot. I don't have time to speak, when in a quick move he lifts me over his shoulder caveman style. When I give a little squeak, he slaps my ass hard. Then he's holding his jeans with the other hand as we make the short walk to the bedroom.

Tossing me onto the bed, he gets right to it, tugging at my jeans. When I squirm, he flips me over and taps my ass. Not too hard, but the sting turns me on. I can tell he's not used to it, but thinks maybe that's what I want. I have to admit, his dominating me is a thrill, so I say nothing lest he stop.

He works my jeans over my hips and surprises me by taking a bite on my ass. I giggle, which gets me another love tap. Once my pants are off, he slides a hand underneath me to raise me up on my knees. Then his tongue is in my pussy. And fuck me if I don't fly to the moon and back. Adding a finger, he's expert enough to easily find the magic button. When I cry out, his mouth and finger are gone.

"Damn, Ryder. You're being a tease."

"And you made me wait for this."

With my eyes closed and my cheek smashed in the mattress, I feel his cock glide between my lips back and forth, but never going inside.

I want to complain, but I sense he wants that, too. So I hold my lips shut. His dick is gone, but his magician fingers are back. Two or three, I'm not sure. Stuffed is how I feel. His other hand rubs circles around my clit, and I get closer to the prize on the other side.

Just as I feel the beginning of an orgasm, the SOB pulls his fingers free.

I can't hold back a curse. "Fuck you, Ryder." I begin to crawl away until he clamps a hand on my shoulder to stop me. Bending over me, his cock nestles between my legs, but not where I need him most.

"If you want me inside you, Gina, you're going to have to beg."

His hand on my chin excites me. I want to tell him what I crave in that second, but I'm afraid he'll freak out over what I have in mind. Instead, I swallow my pride and beg.

"Please put that big cock of yours inside me, Cowboy."

Playfully, he bites down on my ear and then angles his dick at my entrance and slams into me.

Lots of cuss words spill from my lips as I relish the feel of him stretching me. Then it's the sounds of our slapping flesh as he thrusts that makes me get that much closer to the edge.

"Pull my hair," I whisper.

"What?"

"Pull my hair." Tentatively, he does it, but it's not enough. "More," I beg.

The pinpricks of pain heighten everything. The world starts to lose focus, and I'm about to come. Dumb me, I tell him. And my reward is him pulling out while releasing his hold on my hair.

Mad as hell, I flip over and glare at him. He strokes his cock, and I watch for a second, mesmerized. Then I remember where his dick should be. "Orgasm withholding. I didn't think you had it in you. But that's cool. I know how to get myself off."

I draw a line down between my breasts and over the

mound into my core. My back arches as I push two fingers inside myself and moan. His response? He yanks my hand free.

"Mine!"

"Who says?" I challenge.

"Me. And if you want me to fuck you, you'll say it, too."

He reaches up and gently but firmly squeezes my breast while tapping his other hand on my pussy. The tap reminds me I'm deadly close to orgasm. "Tell me whose pussy this is, Gina."

Stubborn as I am, I close my lips together to silence the words from spilling free. His hand leaves my breast and flits across my stomach. His touch is so light, I quiver. Then he stops tapping and circles my nub, but doesn't touch it.

"Fuck you, Ryder. It's yours," I spit.

His smirk precedes him hooking my leg at the knee and pulling me forward. He kneels before me, hiking my butt off the mattress as he plunges into me. A cry escapes my throat. The angle we are at is perfect. I'm so fucking close, I lock my eyes onto his, daring him to deny me again.

Just as things get to the verge of tumbling over, I issue another command as I guide his hand to my throat.

"Squeeze."

His eyes widen in alarm. Just by that, I know he's never done this before. But I need him to now.

"Just do it. I won't die if you let go before I pass out."

He shakes his head.

"Don't be such a pansy. You're going to make me lose it," I complain.

The pansy comment did it. His fingers close around my throat, but not tight enough.

"Tighter, so I can't speak."

Hesitantly he does it, but he's lost his rhythm some.

"Fuck me hard like a real man," I manage to choke out.

His eyes darken, and his thrusts become punishing. His hand bears down and squeezes more to silence me. And not too much longer before stars burst into focus. I relish the leap over into the abyss. His hand leaves my throat, and I suck in air as he takes a few more strokes. Then he grunts his way over the finish line.

He collapses next to me. After catching my breath, I roll over to my side. I'm about to cup his face and kiss him, to say how incredible it was. But the look on his face stops me. My hand in midair drops to my side.

"What's wrong?"

Scrubbing a hand over his face, he says, "I don't think I can do that again."

I fall to my back and stare at the ceiling. "Why?" I ask, not sure I want to hear the answer.

"It felt wrong, like I was hurting you."

Blowing air from my lungs, defeat consumes me. "I'm sorry to be the bearer of bad news, but I like it rough. I warned you from the beginning we weren't compatible."

"Maybe not," he admits.

His words feel like a cleaver has been impaled in my chest. "Why do you need that anyway? Has someone hurt you in the past?"

Yes, but not in the ways he's thinking. So why does his condemnation make me feel dirty?

Pissed off, I say smartly, "I just need it. You'll never understand. And it's cool if it's not your thing."

He sits up and swings his legs over the side of the bed, and I know he's leaving. I almost ask him to take off his shirt, which he never did, just so I can see his fantastic abs one last time.

"You're right. It's not my thing. It's obvious that you don't want to be treated right. I sent you gifts, and you couldn't bother to thank me. Yet, I bet you would thank me now for choking you."

He shakes his head. And without another word, he gets his pants from my floor and leaves my bedroom. I can hear the fabric as he pulls it up. Then it's his feet stepping across the floor. I know he's about to open the door.

"Ryder." He doesn't answer, and that kills me inside. Still, I say what I should have said. "Thank you for the thoughtful gifts."

No *you're welcome* comes, just the sound of the door closing as he exits my life. Tears spill from my eyes, and I can't recall the last time I cried like this. Why did him leaving hurt so much? I barely know the man. Then again, some people make an impression in your life.

When Cassie came up to me in grade school and declared we were going to be friends, there was never any doubt.

The only thing I doubt now is that I might have let the best man who ever entered my life, even over my old man who gave me life and nothing more, walk out my door.

RYDER

isorientation smacks me in the face when I wake up the next morning. It takes me a few minutes to figure out I'm on Fletcher and Cassie's sofa. Good thing it's a huge sectional or I'd have the worst stiff neck known to man. My head clangs with the aftereffects of tequila, and I have a major freak out about the fact that I drove out here in my inebriated state. Rolling off the sofa, I stumble into the kitchen for some badly needed hydration, and that's when I see it.

Here are your keys. Car is parked outside. Didn't want you taking any chances in your condition. Sam

Thank God. Sam drove me home. I need to send him some tickets or something. What the hell was I thinking getting so hammered last night? Then the memories nail me. *Gina.*

Jesus fuck me. What the hell is up with that woman? Is she really as messed up as that? The idea of someone hurting her makes me want to jam my fist through a wall. I can do wild and rough, but choking? So not my thing. That is totally out of my league. It freaked the hell out of me. Spanking, hell yeah. Sexy as fuck. Toys—I am one hundred percent on board for those. That sex swing—totally hot as shit. I'm game on for all that, but choking is a hard limit—isn't that what they call it—for me. And it's a goddamn pisser because I can't get her out of my mind. Fucking Gina.

No use rubbing this shit in. I take a quick shower and make sure the place is as spotless as it was when I got here. Then I hit the road. I need to have my ass in gear for practice in the morning. We have a few days until our next game, but we're winding the regular season down, and it's time to be on point here. Focus is never more important than it is now.

Riley is serving up a pile of scrambled eggs when I walk in the door. God, I'm starving. All that alcohol from the night before just reminded me how hungry I am.

"Any left?" I ask.

"Mmm, sorry, no."

Dropping my keys onto the counter, I head straight for the fridge and pull out the eggs, milk, sausage, and everything else I need for a monster omelet. Riley eyes me the entire time.

"Where were you last night?"

"Waynesville."

"Did you see Gina?" Her eyes gleam with interest.

"Yeah."

"Well? Did she love all her presents?"

"I wouldn't know." I don't look at my sister as I continue to make my breakfast. She doesn't say a word in response, and when my food is ready, I plate it and take a seat at the counter.

"Spill it all, Ryder."

Here's the thing. I love my sister and share a lot with her. But no way to the fucking hell am I giving her any of these sordid details.

"Nothing to share." I keep eating.

"Liar. You're hiding something. You really like her, and for you to act like this after everything you did for her, something's up."

"Hmm mmm."

"Come on, Ryder. I can help you. I'm your sister."

I swallow the last bite of food and put my plate into the dishwasher. "Listen, I appreciate what you're trying to do, but you said it yourself. You don't want to get stuck in the middle. Leave it alone, Riley."

"But I don't get it. She didn't like the spa thing?" My sister wears confusion well. And I'll admit, it baffled the shit out of me, too. Who wouldn't like a spa gift certificate, especially the one I loaded up for Gina?

"Can't say. Let me tell you this much, and then we drop the Gina subject. She wouldn't answer my calls, so I don't know if she loved or hated it."

"Now that's fucking rude as hell. How much did you spend on it?"

"That's not the point."

"No, but I'm curious."

"Five hundred."

"I don't get it. She doesn't seem the type to be so ungracious."

"Think again, sis. She is."

"I'm sorry. No wonder she never returned my calls when I wanted to ask her to one of your games. Guess I was wrong about her."

"So was I," I say, heading to my room.

A few hours later, I drive to the practice field. We have a team meeting first, and then we hit it. Since the season is winding down, I need to give it my all. I should have never poured all that liquor into me last night. My game is going to be off, and if I have any ideas of becoming the starting pitcher, or ace as it's called, I need to pull my ass together and forget Gina. She's only fucking up my livelihood now, and that's not good.

When I enter the team room, I'm one of the last to arrive, which sucks. The manager gives me one of his head-to-toe scans, and I'm not sure I like his assessment. He sees what I don't want him to—a poorly disguised hungover pitcher.

"Okay, ladies, we have a few items to cover, and then Ms. Whitestone will be joining us. First, we only have a handful of home games left and the same for aways. We're this close," he pinches his thumb and forefinger together, "to the playoffs. I believe right here," he pounds his chest so hard you can hear the thump, "we have as good a chance as any team out there of making it. Who's with me on this?" The room breaks out into a riotous cheer. One thing about our manager is he can sure get the team riled up in a good way. He lets us go on until we're hollered out. "Remember, this is not a singular effort. We all need each other in order to make this happen." His gray eyes land on me, and guilt instantly floods me. He has this way of making you want to do your absolute best in every possible situation. And there I went and pulled a damn drunk last night. He knows it, too. I nod gravely, and now we're on the same page.

He gives us a rundown of what's going to occur for the next few days and how our scheduling is going to run as far as practices go.

"Do I have everyone's firm commitment to stay straight here, to be level-headed, and to give it your goddamned all?"

Another ear-splitting cheer fills the room as the guys pound whatever they can get their feet and legs on. When he finishes, Ms. Whitestone steps into the room to a round of applause.

"Gentlemen, thank you. And thank you for a monumental season so far. But let's take it a step further. Let's bring home the Commissioner's Trophy this year by winning the World Series." A round of applause breaks out that rivals the cheers our manager received. "To win it our first year would be amazing, and you know what that would mean not only for us, but for the city of Charlotte and the Carolinas as well. Let's make them proud to be a Cougars fan."

The cheers go on and on, and I'm caught up in the moment of excitement. This is a banner year for us, and my exhilaration grows.

When the noise settles down, she yells out, "Let's go practice ball, gentlemen."

The men filter out of the room, and as I walk past her, she says, "Ryder, may I have a word, please?"

"Sure, Ms. Whitestone." I stop in front of her, and she smiles.

"Let's go to my office where we can talk in private."

What the fuck? Am I getting fired? I wasn't that drunk last night and didn't get arrested or anything.

"Sure thing." I tag along behind her like a dutiful pup.

When we get to one of the private offices, which isn't her bona fide fancy office that's located in the executive building for the team, she tells me to take a seat. I'm sweating bullets, which smells mildly—okay, heavily of whiskey laced with tequila—and she begins to yammer on about how great my season has been. And I wait for the big *but*.

"But, Ryder, you could be in a better place by now." When I don't respond, she adds, "If you know what I mean."

"No, ma'am, I don't quite follow you."

"I believe there is a long future here for you and this franchise." She licks her lips. "We could make a hell of a team."

Oh, my fucking balls. And I'm not talking baseballs. Is the Queen of the Cougars flirting with me? No, I take that back. Is my boss hitting on me? My nuts climb up my ass because the last thing I could possibly do is her. I think my tequila wants out. As in barf.

"Oh?" Yeah, like that's a good response. Right? I'll play the dumb athlete.

"Yes, in fact, escorting me to a fundraiser can help you as much as the team. Get your name out there, so reporters aren't surprised when in the near future it's announced you've become the Cougars' ace. How does that sound?"

Escort? Fundraiser? That doesn't sound too bad as long as it doesn't come down to any removal of clothing. I can handle that.

"Fundraiser?"

"Yes, I like to donate to the Kids Without Homes charity, and every year they have a gala. One of the things I want to do is bring one of the players because it will show their involvement. You, of course, would be required to give a donation."

"Oh, of course." Relief washes through me. "How much? Ten thousand enough?"

She laughs, and it reminds me of Tinkerbell. "Why, Ryder, that's terribly generous of you."

Here I thought she wanted me to fuck her. Hell, I'd give twenty grand to avoid having to do that chore.

"I'm happy to give to a great cause such as that. When is it?"

She smiles, and her Chiclet teeth nearly blind me. "This Saturday."

"I'll put it on my calendar. Is it black tie?"

"Actually, it's not because some of the kids go. But you will need to wear something nice, though not a suit."

"Got it covered. Shall I pick you up?"

That Tinkerbell laugh fills the room again. "Gracious no. I'll send the limo around to pick you up. Say six-ish. And thank you." She pats my hand, and her long lacquered nails look a bit creepy to me. They remind me of talons. I'm so glad Gina doesn't wear all that shit on her nails. Not that it matters because I'm done with her anyway.

"Oh, and, Ryder, if you didn't take my hint, you can expect to start coming up in the next game or two."

"Thank you, ma'am, but I would've done this anyway." And I would have. I'm all about helping the kids.

Keeping true to Ms. Whitestone's word, my pitching coach has hinted if we make it to the playoffs I will be the ace. I start the following game, and pitch well. I'm relieved in the sixth inning, and my arm is iced and rested, even though it feels great. A pitcher is usually only allowed between ninety to a hundred twenty pitches per game, so the manager thought it best to pull me after ninety-five. He didn't want to stress my arm, and I'm good with that. We go on to win, which is all I can ask for.

On Saturday, Ms. Whitestone picks me up, and when I get in the limo, she asks me to call her Regina. "It's better for the event if we're on a first-name basis. It seems less formal that way."

"I can do that, but when we're in front of the team, I prefer to stick to Ms. Whitestone if that's okay."

"Yes, that's fine."

We enter the gala, and the room is decorated with all kinds of kid stuff from toys and games, to athletic jerseys, to colorful pictures on the walls. Our team is well represented, which makes me proud to be a Cougar.

As soon as we enter, camera flashes go off everywhere, and reporters approach us as the local news channels interview us. Ms. Whitestone handles most of the questions, as she's the experienced one here, but then the focus turns to me and the win from the last games I pitched. I'm in the spotlight now. It's a paparazzi-fest, and when we're able to shake free of them, my phone blows up.

Riley texts me telling me to check Instagram, Facebook, and Twitter. When I open my accounts, there's my face next to Regina's looking like we're on the happiest of dates. Her arm is around my waist, and mine is around hers. She's quite the snappy cougar, and I don't mean the baseball team. Her smile is megawatt, and she gazes at me as I stare at the camera. Surely this was taken as I was being interviewed, but she looks like a lovesick goon. Christ.

My phone goes off again. It's Riley telling me that if Gina see this, she's going to think I have a new girlfriend. Fuck my life. Then Fletcher texts, along with Cassidy. What the hell is going on?

Fletcher: *Dude. Tired of women your own age?*
Cassidy: *What the hell, R?*

The next one comes from Gina. I'm surprised to hear from her. She couldn't take time out of her busy life to thank me for all the goddamn gifts I sent her, yet as soon as I go to a fundraiser, which is clearly seen everywhere, she's happy to get in touch then.

I see you've found a woman who is more up to your speed. Wishing you all the happiness in the world. Gina

A red haze floats over my eyes, and I excuse myself from Regina's presence. I have an urgent need to punch the shit out of something. Only I can't because there is nothing around to destroy, and I won't risk injuring myself. So I suck it up and try to gain control of my temper. Of all the shitty things to do. I'm at a fucking fundraiser for kids for fuck's sake, and she can't see past her little petty jealousies. I never pegged Gina as mean-spirited, but this takes it to an all-time low.

There's one way to retaliate. Using my phone, I snap several photos of what the charity is and some of the kids who are present. Then I send her the photos and a text back.

Indeed I have. It's someone who gives a damn about children without homes and who raises money for them. I offered to help, and this is who I'm spending my evening with. And btw, she thanked me for what I've done, unlike someone I know. Ryder

I hit send before I change my mind. However, it does nothing to ease my anger. Regina recognizes something is wrong, but I brush it aside and get through the event. As soon as it's over, we leave. She thanks me profusely and wants to know if she can count on me for another event for Kids Without Homes.

"I'm all in. Whatever you need."

When we get to my place, I just about hop out of the car before it stops. There's something I'm going to do, and I don't give a damn how late it is. I don't even bother going inside. My car is parked in the garage provided for condo owners, so that's where I head. I hit the road. Destination: Gina's apartment.

The Dirty Hammer is still open when I pull into town. It makes me wonder if she's working. If she is, I'll have to wait. But I go around back and take the stairs up. After I pound on the door, I wait.

"Sam, I told you I wanted the night off," she says, opening the door.

I push my way in, saying, "Sorry, it's not Sam. And we need to set some things straight. One, you don't have the right to jump to those kinds of conclusions about me. Two, why are you so mean-spirited? And three," I pull her against me, "I'm here to accept your thanks for the gifts I sent that you so rudely never gave me." And my mouth crashes onto hers as I grasp a handful of her disarrayed hair and twist it around my fingers. I back her into the closest wall, hips holding her prisoner, and say, "Tell me to stop."

Her chest heaves as she locks gazes with mine. "No. Because I don't want you to."

"I won't leave, and there'll be no choking ever again."

"O-okay."

"I'm game for all kinds of shit, Gina, but not that."

She nods.

"On your knees. I want my dick in your mouth. Because it's all I thought of the whole way here."

Gina falls to her knees and rips my pants open. I'm hard as stone, and my cock springs out as her mouth latches on. Her lips wrap around me, and she slides up and down while grasping the base of me as she squeezes. Fuck, she gives great head.

"Suck. Hard."

She takes direction well, too. Her hand cups my balls, and her fingers tighten around them in a soft rhythm. Then her mouth takes them in and I want her to stop, but I don't.

"Enough. I want to see your pussy. On your dining room table. And take your clothes off."

She shimmies out of her cami and yoga pants, then walks backwards to her table and sits on it.

"Legs up, feet flat on the table. Spread yourself wide for me so I can see you."

Without a word, she obeys. I like this Gina.

"Rub yourself. All around. Are you wet?"

"Yes." Her voice is a husky whisper.

"You aren't even close to where I'm taking you. Make yourself come. Now. Fast."

Her hand works fast, moving over her clit in a rapid

motion. I nearly make her stop because I'm about to bust a nut. She climaxes in a soft moan, her head thrown back, and I want so badly to kiss her mouth, only I don't. I hold back.

Rolling a condom on, I hold my cock and rub it up and down over her slit. I repeat this over and over. Placing her feet on my shoulders, I say, "Eyes over here," and I point to where my cock is. I slap her clit with my dick. She moans. I keep that up until she's writhing around, and then I plunge inside her.

"I want your pussy stretched around me until you scream when you come." With relentless strokes, I intend to keep that promise to her. Her pebbled nipples arch toward me, so I pinch and twist them as she grinds her hips into me. When I get close, my thumb presses on her clit, and reaching beneath her, I slide a finger into her ass. She screams my name as she comes, and I shoot off around the same time, pumping my orgasm into her. Or I should say into the condom.

"One of these days, I'm going to fuck you bare, Gina."

She only stares, but her eyes are as soft as I've ever seen them. Her hand reaches for mine, and she mutters, "I think I'm going to sleep for days."

"Sleep? You think that was it? We've only begun."

GINA

Knots in my stomach form as he watches me. I try not to squirm under his intense stare.

"What?" I finally ask.

His thumb brushes over my lip. "I like it when you're happy."

"Happy?"

"Don't frown."

I don't realize that I've done it until after I let the smile slip from my face. The vulnerability he creates in me scares me shitless. The little girl in me remembers when my dad would promise to take me someplace only to have a *change of plans* when some woman came calling he found more interesting. And I don't want to feel that pain ever again. The fact is no man ever has put me first. I can't delude myself into thinking this man will, at least not for long. So I remove his hand from my face and try to wiggle free.

"Stop."

I glare at him, but pinned as I am, I can't go anywhere.

"What do you want from me?" I question.

"Maybe this is a hard concept for you, but I want more than this, Gina."

What? He wants to put me on lock so that I'm his until he's done with me. His sister's warning from that first time I met her is clear. Ryder doesn't do relationships any more than I do.

"I'm not a fairy fucking princess, Ryder. I've got nothing more to offer you than this. But I do owe you a thank you for all you did." I spread my arms to encompass the room. The organization of things is evidence enough of some of what he did for me. "The flowers, the spa gift certificate, which I can't accept by the way, and you see the bookshelves and all."

His expert hand slides between my legs and strokes my slit, firing me up to life. "I would gift you the stars just to see them twinkle in your eyes because you're more than this, Gina. More than the sum of your experiences. I know you don't believe me, and someone in your life should pay for not letting you know how much more you are than this."

He glides two fingers inside me, and my back bows in response.

"I can give you this." Curling his finger, he accesses my inner magic button. With my eyes heavenward, I barely make out his next words. "Or treat you like a fairy fucking princess. Because that's what I fucking see, Gina, a dream."

Mercilessly, he fills me with a third finger, and every nerve ending in my body is ignited. Abruptly, he stops, pulling free. "What's it going to be?"

"Stop." I roll to my stomach annoyed at his tactics, but he doesn't give up.

He moves, and his heat covers my back. The heavy weight of his length presses deliciously at my opening. I can't say I don't want it because I most certainly do.

"We're not sexually compatible," I toss out.

His lips blaze a trail up my neck, causing me to shiver. As he pushes inside me, he says, "Your body says otherwise."

A firm hand cups my center and angling me expertly for him to work my nub and slowly thrust inside me. I see fucking stars as my vision blurs when he says, "I want you at my games, cheering me on like a fucking champ, wearing my jersey, telling the world you're my girl."

I can only moan because surely Ryder isn't talking this way.

"This is my pussy, and you're my girlfriend until we can make this fucking permanent."

Shock has my mouth opening. He angles his head and captures my mouth in a soul-searing kiss.

When I come the next time, I howl like a fucking banshee. I must have been loud as shit because a thump comes from the floor. Sam must have used a broom to tap on the ceiling from downstairs.

A giggle, a fucking giggle, escapes me like I'm some

little girl.

"That's what I want to see," he says.

Immediately, I frown. "This will never work."

He sighs. "Dammit, Gina. What do I have to do? Screw your brains out until you get it through your thick skull that we are going to do this?"

His softening cock is still inside me, but I don't dare move. I love the feeling of him there.

"How is this going to work? Have you ever had a girlfriend before?"

"I have."

It's telling that he doesn't elaborate. "And?"

"And what? It didn't work out."

Pursing my lips, I say, "And why didn't it work out? Did you get bored?"

He's quick to answer, "Not exactly."

I grind my teeth because he's not being forthright. "It's called communication. If you want to even try this, we have to be honest with each other."

"Fine." There's a lengthy pause, but I refuse to fill it. "She didn't get the concept of monogamy."

A laugh bursts from my chest, and I don't mean to when I notice his frown. I turn with him still pressed somewhat on top of me. "Sorry, that's not funny. But that didn't jade you against relationships?"

He shrugs. "It makes me leery, but I don't put other people's bullshit on someone else. When I look at you, I don't see a vindictive lying bitch. I see a dark-haired beauty who is probably just as fucking scared about being hurt as I am."

The nail is struck on the head by a hammer. Why does he have to look so fucking adorable when he says it, too?

"And what happens when I want to have a threesome?" I pronounce. As expected, his eyes pop from his head. "Down, boy. I don't mean another girl."

His lips pinch in a tight line. "You want to fuck two guys?"

"What? You say it like that's unheard of. Can you tell me you haven't with two girls?" He starts to speak, but I hold up a hand to stop him. "Don't answer. I don't want to know."

That elicits a smile on his face. "Jealous?"

"Not necessarily jealous. But my point is, you think it's cool for a guy to do two girls, but a girl with two guys is like taboo and shit?"

"It's not that. Let me be fucking honest. I'm jealous. The idea of another guy touching you gives me hives. I might need to take a Benadryl for even thinking it."

That provokes a laugh I can't stop.

"We can play with all the toys you want to give you that double penetration, but I'm never going to share you."

Then he's on me. If there is one thing I've learned in this short time is the man is insatiable. Without me even answering, I have a boyfriend. In fact, somewhere in the early morning, he kisses me and tells me he has to get to practice. And like the girlfriend I've become, I miss him, his warmth, but doze off knowing he'll be back because he's mine. *Mine*. Somehow he cracked my protective shell, and even though I feel as naked as an M&M without the candy coating, his sweet center is worth the risk.

The next day, I realize I haven't even told Ryder about the letter I received from my birth mom. What freaks me is that I thought of telling him before Cassie. I leave a frantic message on her phone for her to call me. There are so many things I need to tell her.

After, I place a much delayed call to Riley.

"It's too freaking early in the morning. It better be important. Who is this?"

"Gina," I say with deference.

The pause is so long, for a second I think she's hung up.

"Gina," she replies.

"Look, I'm sorry I haven't called back. Life got busy, and at first I didn't recognize the number, but the California area code that matched Ryder's clued me in. But those are excuses. Truth is, I was scared. Things were complicated between your brother and me."

"Complicated?"

"Yeah, but we've worked it out, and I owe you an apology. I should have called."

"Maybe, but truth is, we weren't really friends yet. You owed me nothing. I appreciate your call. In the future, whatever happens with you and my brother stays with you guys. If we are going to be friends, we have to remember that."

"Agreed."

"Well, if that's all, I need sleep."

"Actually, I wanted to know if you would join me at the spa."

She agrees before practically hanging up on me. Apparently, she's not a morning person. Neither am I, but it's almost afternoon, I laugh as I think to myself. Then, I get ready for work.

Later that night, Mark shows up on my barstool with frustrated eyes.

"What will it be?" I ask, planting my elbows on the bar.

"A drink and a friend."

Mark is like my next best friend to Cassie, and something isn't right. He's usually the one giving me a pep talk, not the other way around.

I pour him two fingers of Jameson. "What happened?"

It's a while before he answers. "Lost my job."

I have to stop in the middle of making a Skittle for another customer.

"What the hell?" Mark is an amazing financial investor. I can't believe he got canned.

"It isn't me. The whole company failed. Apparently, I was the only one producing. And even my clients can't maintain an entire company."

He swallows the Jameson like water, and not judging him I pour another.

"What's the plan?" Because I know he has a backup plan. He always prepared for everything.

His shoulders lift in defeat. That rattles me because there is no way he's in financial trouble.

"I've got money to last for a while until I find something, but you and I both know there is nothing around here."

My chest constricts, and I feel the unwelcome prick of tears in my eyes. If Marks leaves, I'll have no one. Cassie is gone for the most part, although she should be in town tomorrow to make office hours.

"I don't want to leave the area," he adds.

I clamp my lips shut before I agree with him. I love him enough to not want to hold him back, even if I'll be left behind, yet again.

"You do what you have to do."

"There is this company, Rhoades Investment, in Charleston. They've been courting me to open a satellite office in Charlotte for years."

He shrugs again. Having a hard time digesting his potential leaving causes me to over serve him. At the end of the night, I haul him upstairs to my apartment and unceremoniously dump him on my bed and pull off his shoes. Tired myself, I fall in bed next to him, fully dressed. It's not a big deal because he's like the brother I never had. What happened between us happened when we were teens and caused us to come to the same conclusion that we were better off as friends.

So when I wake to the sound of knocking at my door,

I think nothing of it. I get up and call out, "Hold your horses!" thinking it's Cassie stopping by before she starts working for the day. She probably feels bad she didn't call me back.

Only I find Ryder at my door with something that smells yummy. I focus on the steamy travel mug of coffee and the brown bag as I let him smooth back my hair. Stupidly, I feel girlish that he sees me with bedhead. And when has that ever happened?

I push my hair back when I hear Mark. He'd been in my shower when I'd gone to open the door. I get a glimpse of him as he steps bare-chested and damp before Ryder goes postal.

The moment to stop Ryder's forward progress with fist raised is lost to me as I watch in horror as he cracks Mark's jaw.

"No," I scream, but it's too late.

RYDER

F ury blinds me as Mark walks out of the bathroom. Every coherent thought leaves me as motion overrides everything. One, two, three steps later, and my fist connects with his jaw. I don't even feel it against my knuckles, and I don't see him fall back against the wall. What brings me out of my anger-trance is Gina's scream. It comes from a tunnel through the thick haze of rage. Then, when I move to fire off another jab, her hand grabs my arm, and for some wild reason, I stop and turn. Her mouth is moving, but I can barely hear what she's saying.

"Ryder! Ryder! Ryder!"

She shakes me, this time hard.

"Ryder!" My name echoes throughout her tiny apartment.

"It's Mark! He's my best friend next to Cassie. He's like my brother. Stop! Please!" The clenching hand on my arm, the pleading edge to her voice, all converge and punch through the wall of insanity that grips me. My chest heaves, and I slowly, slowly regain my composure.

"Fuck, fuck, fuck," I mutter. I can't believe I just knocked the shit out of Fletcher's best friend. What the hell!

Gina runs to Mark's aid, who leans against the wall, massaging his jaw. "Are you okay?" her soft voice asks him.

"I'll live. This isn't the first time I've taken one to the face. But damn, Gina, you should've warned me you had such a jealous boyfriend." His playful tone flies right over her head.

"I would have had I known. But, don't worry, he's not my boyfriend."

"Oh, yes, he is," I say. "And, Mark, my apologies, man. Sorry for going crazy train on you, but seeing a half-naked dude in my girl's place didn't sit too well with me."

"Hey, I'm with you. I wouldn't go for that either. But I was over served last night," he glances at her, "so Gina dragged my drunk as hell ass up here so I wouldn't get killed trying to drive home. And honestly, I passed out and don't even remember. I was drowning my sorrows, and I paid for it." He rubs his jaw and works it around a little.

"Sorrows? Or am I being too nosy?"

"Nah, my company has taken a huge hit, so they're closing up shop and I've lost my job."

"Oh, that sucks, man. Sorry to hear it."

"Yeah, hence the drunk-fest."

Now I really feel like shit. "And here I go adding a little extra on top of it all."

Gina, not one to let it pass so easily, says, "Yeah. Real nice of you, Cowboy."

But, I'm not going to let it go either. Pulling her up to me, I say, "Well, it's all your fault, fairy princess."

I want to laugh at the face she makes. She reminds me of my pet goldfish I had when I was a kid. Her mouth opens and closes, opens and closes. Finally, she says, "How is it my fault?"

I'm going all in for this. "Several reasons. One, if you weren't so damn beautiful, I wouldn't be all hot and bothered. Two, if you weren't my girl, I wouldn't give a shit who was in this apartment with you. Three, if it wasn't for that sassy mouth of yours, I wouldn't want to kiss you all the time. Four, if you didn't have such a big heart and didn't give a shit about your friends and the people you care about, I wouldn't be here in the first place."

She blinks, not once but several times, and it's clear I've rattled her to the core. Then she wriggles that sexy body away from mine and says, "I need to get Mark some ice." Her voice has suddenly gotten a bit hoarse. Indeed, I've hit my target.

Mark clears his throat, grabbing my attention. When I glance at him, I laugh. He's given me not one, but two thumbs-up. And then he stage whispers, "It's about damn time."

I mumble back, "I really am sorry about the..." I circle my finger around my jaw, indicating the jab.

He shrugs it off. "I'll live, man."

Gina comes back with a baggie filled with ice. "Are we gonna stand in the hall all morning, or would you all like to join me in the living room?"

We follow the leader to take seats in her still uncluttered living room. I smile about that. She eyes me suspiciously, but I only shake my head.

"So, how about that breakfast I brought you?" I ask.

"Well, since there are three of us, I'd feel guilty eating it in front of everyone."

Mark, who looks a bit green, says, "Count me out for any food. I am under the hangover weather this morning. All I want is ice water for now."

"I already ate, so go for it, my little fairy princess." I grin.

She scowls, but grabs the bag and digs in. When she sees the warm cinnamon scones inside, the scowl disappears. "Oh, my." One bite and a whole bunch of *Mmmms* later, I believe I may be back on solid ground again.

"So, Cowboy, what brings you to these parts?" she asks.

"I thought that would be fairly obvious."

From her sly grin, she's going in a completely different direction than where I intended. Although, I'm not opposed to that, but with Mark here, it makes it a little difficult.

"No, you're missing something." I point to the bag I dropped when my moment of insanity overruled the purpose of my visit. It's on the floor near the entrance of the apartment.

She stops chewing on her scone, and now the curiosity hits her. "What is it?"

"Guess you're going to have to open it to find out."

Mark says, "I think it's time for me to get out of here."

Holding up a palm, I say, "Hang on a sec."

"You sure? This might be cozy time for you two."

Laughing, I say, "It might be, but just wait. You'll see why in a minute."

Gina's finished her scone and sets her coffee down. Her sassy mouth says, "A good cowboy would bring that bag over to his fairy princess."

"Yeah, but a good fairy princess would use fairy dust to zap that bag over to herself." She laughs, and I end up getting the bag and hand delivering it to her with an elaborate bow.

"Your wish, my command."

She greedily grabs the bag and pulls out the contents. When she sees what's inside, a smile that could light up the damn ball field breaks across her face.

"It's your jersey!"

"Yeah. All for you, my fairy princess. Hand delivered for the game this week. Plus, two tickets in the box. For you and a friend. That's where you come in, Mark. That is, if you want to after I decked you."

There are also two Cougars hats inside the bag, and her hand pulls those out, and she tosses one to Mark. "Are you in?" she asks him.

"Hell yeah. I'd love to go. It's not like my schedule is packed, but even if it were, I'd clear it for this. Which hotel do I need to get a reservation in?"

"Nah, you can stay at my place. It's huge. I have two extra bedrooms, so there is more than enough room."

"Is Riley going?" Gina asks.

"No, she's playing in a tournament in Hawaii."

"Wow. Tough life," Gina says.

"Actually, it is. She's been traveling like crazy. And her caddy told her after this season ends, he wants out of his contract. So now she's not only busy as shit with her schedule, she's on the hunt for a new caddy, which really sucks."

Gina scrunches up her mouth. "Ouch. That's fucked."

"Yeah, so she's in a bad funk. But Riley is Riley. She'll make it work. And knowing her, she'll come out on top."

"I hope so. So, we can both stay with you then?" Gina wants to know.

"Absolutely. Count on that. Since it's an afternoon game, we can grab dinner and go out afterward. I don't have a Sunday game. We're off, so it'll be a great night."

Gina looks at Mark. "You in?"

"Don't ask me twice."

Mark gets up and heads to Gina's bedroom to get dressed. When he emerges, he tells Gina he'll be in touch so they can finalize their plan for the game. He and

125

I shake hands, and he leaves.

"Jesus, Ryder, I thought we were gonna be taking him to the hospital."

"Yeah, sorry I lost it like that." I glance at my hand, knowing I'm going to hear it from Coach. "But let me ask you something. If you showed up at my place and a chick walked out of the bathroom half-naked, what would your reaction be?"

"Okay, I'd want to scratch her eyes out. I'm not sure if I would, but I'd want to."

Pulling her onto my lap, I run my finger down her cheek. Her hair is a tangled mess and looks like we just had a sexathon. I love her like this. Rubbing my thumb over her lower lip, I say, "You have two passes on guys up here. Mark and Sam. Anybody else is a dead man."

"What about Fletcher?"

"Fletcher, too. But that's it."

Her lower lip doesn't stand a chance against my mouth. She offers zero resistance. Instead, she leans into me, and I inhale her sigh. Gina is softness wrapped up in a package of sass. She believes herself to be tough and unyielding, but that's not what she is at all. Underneath that Plexiglas wall she's created, she's tenderhearted, kind, caring, and loving. I'm going to destroy that damn barrier and show her exactly who and what she is, even if it destroys me in the process.

She pulls her sexy-as-fuck mouth away from mine and says, "So, does that mean only Fletcher, Mark, and Sam are allowed up here?"

"That's right."

She scrambles off my lap and says, "Then I guess I'm going to have to ask you to leave, Cowboy. I don't want to break any rules." She wears that sexy smirk I love.

Standing, I pick her up and carry her to the bedroom. "You know damn well what I meant. And just for that, I'm going to punish you." I slide off her pants and give her ass a good slap. She squeals. "You weren't supposed to like that, Gina. Guess I didn't give you a good enough spanking. On your knees."

She quickly obliges. My hand makes contact with her ass, and it becomes pink. I massage the smooth as silk skin, and feel the warmth beneath my palm. Then I give her another swat. She moans, and my dick hardens. This isn't working for me. The sight of her ass and bare pussy before me is more than I can stand, so using both hands, I widen her stance on the bed. Then I drop to my knees and bury my face in her sweet cunt. Honey. That's what they should call this. She tastes exactly like it. My tongue swipes her long and deep, and then it flicks her clit as my fingers sink into her. Hooking them, I hit the spot that sets her off. Gina is a moaner, but she doesn't do it in an over exaggerated way. Her sounds are soft, sensual, and so arousing that I wouldn't have to see her to get a hard-on. But add the visual and what a fucking bonus.

She comes in all her glory, and I roll on a condom as fast as I can because I want to feel those little muscles squeezing my dick. I know I can make her come again, but to sink into her, as she's orgasming is the most phenomenal sensation my dick has ever experienced. Too bad he can't speak for himself. My holding power is minimal. I try, but at least I wait until she's had climax number two. And then I empty myself into her. Or the condom as it is.

When I'm milked dry, I pull out and get rid of the necessary evil. Then I flop back in bed and pull her on top of me. "Do you know how many times I jack off thinking about you? Do you know how often my dick is like a damn piece of wood because I'm thinking about you?"

She doesn't answer. All she does is nuzzle my neck.

"Gina, do you ever masturbate when you think of me?"

Still not looking at me, she mumbles her throaty response into my neck, "Yeah."

"Do you use your hand? Or one of your little toys?" I'm grinning, but she can't see me.

"Both."

"Do you do it a lot or only once in a while?"

"A lot."

"How often, Gina. Every day?"

"Maybe." Her tone is squeaky, which is surprising for the usually bold Gina. I pull her up to face me.

"Why so shy? I think it's fucking hot that you get yourself off thinking of me. A lot. And I don't care how you do it."

"I don't know. It's personal, maybe?"

Brushing her hair away from her face, I say, "Yeah, like me telling you I jack off constantly when I think of you?"

"That's totally hot."

"See? Don't ever shy away from me."

The Gina I know comes back to life. "I'm not shy." And with that, she punches me in the arm. Gratefully, not my right one.

"Ow. That hurt."

She laughs. "It did not."

"Kiss it and make it better."

She puckers up her lips and kisses my arm. I'm a bit surprised she did it. "I have someplace else that needs a kiss because it's a little sore, too."

Her shoulders shake as she tries to hide her laughter. But without speaking, she wriggles down the bed, and before I know it, I'm the recipient of the best blow job ever. My fingers furrow into her hair as she takes me deep and sucks me off to the point of me coming. When I give her the little head tap, she never breaks stride. Or should I say suck. I'm blowing it into her throat and pumping into her like a piston. Fuck. Me. Senseless.

I know one thing. I think I'm in love.

GINA

Staring at the door like a lovesick puppy, I feel deliciously used. The man can fuck like a bull but last way longer than eight seconds. Is that why I was so attracted to him?

Later that day, I meet Riley at the spa. We're sitting in the massaging chairs getting pedicures when Riley changes topics.

"Look, I'm just going to be straight up."

Shit. I say nothing for a second, trying to figure out why she's pissed. "Riley—"

"My brother is into you. And I get it, even though you're not his usual type."

"Hold up—"

"I'm not saying you aren't pretty enough, but he usually dates clueless groupies. Actually, I wouldn't call it dating. The last girl who had a brain was way too into his status."

"You should know—"

But the girl is on a roll. "He told me the other day he's practicing like shit lately, and that the coaches have noticed. And I can't have you ruining his chances of becoming the starting pitcher. That's been his dream for as long as I can remember."

"I think you have this all wrong."

But she's not hearing me.

"What I had wrong was you. Just tell my brother you're not interested so he can move on."

I like Riley, but I'm not going to put up with this. "You know what?"

"What?" she answers, finally giving me a chance to speak.

Meanwhile, everyone in hearing distance watches us with Ping-Pong glances.

"You're like a Rottweiler with a bone. Your brother and I are a thing."

"A thing?"

I let out a half-laugh.

"He calls himself my boyfriend." Her shoulders relax, and for once she has nothing to say. So I fill the space between us. "Look, I get you want to protect him, but if anyone needs protecting it's me. Further, you're the one with the rules about not being in the middle of his and my thing. Trust me, he can handle himself. Otherwise, I couldn't be with him."

"You're right. I'm sorry. I'm under a lot of pressure."

"Wow," I say.

"I'm not too proud to admit when I'm wrong. And

frankly, I'm happy because I think you and I can be good friends." Her voice changes. "Does this mean you're not going to take me to a sex club?"

A bubble of laugher chokes me. "Absolutely we're going to a sex club. I'll be in Charlotte in a few days to go to Ryder's next home game."

"Damn, I have a tourney. We may have to find time to go when the season is over."

We bump fists. I really like her.

"So, if we're going to be friends, you have to tell me. Are you dating anyone?"

Her eyes sparkle. She leans over and whispers, "I wouldn't call it formal or anything, but there is this guy on the circuit I've been messing around with off and on."

Time flies when we're having fun. And too soon, we are trading hugs. It's when I'm alone I'm reminded what it's been like not having Cassie around.

Not having heard from her, I head over to her office, hoping to catch her. But I find out she's not there. I'm told she's in town, but had to call out sick. That's not like her at all. And no fucking phone call.

Her car is out in front of their house. When I knock on the door, I get no answer. That freaks me the fuck out. Luckily, I have a key. I use it and go inside. Only, calling out her name gets no response.

Two at a time, I climb the stairs. I find her passed out on the bathroom floor. My heart races as I call her name.

"Cassie!"

Her eyes blink and focus on me. "What happened?"

Crouching down, I brush back her hair. "I don't know. You tell me."

She presses her fingertips to her forehead. "I haven't felt well. I've just been so damn tired. I couldn't keep anything down, and I felt dizzy."

Pressing the back of my hand to her head, she doesn't feel warm, but I don't know shit about this type of thing.

"I should call 911 or Fletcher."

With sudden strength, she sits up. "No. Don't. I'm fine. And Fletcher's on a plane and he'll just worry. I feel better. Just a little hungry."

I help her stand, but she's not exactly steady. She ends up only making it as far as her bed.

"Cassie, don't be stubborn. You should see a doctor."

Biting her lip, she says, "It's like one of two things."

"What's that?"

There is a long pause. "It's either some stomach bug or... I'm pregnant."

My eyes grow wide. "You're pregnant."

It's not even a question. She nods. "I think so. That's why I went into the bathroom to take a test, but I got dizzy before I could take it."

"Stay here."

In there, I find the unopened box. Back in her room, I plop down next to her.

Maybe you should eat and drink something first. Let me fix you something to eat. Her eyes grow in alarm.

"Oh my God. I'm not that bad of a cook."

Pursing her lips together, she almost turns green.

"I can make you some soup and bring you crackers."

She nods. I venture downstairs and find a can of classic Campbell's Chicken Noodle soup in her cabinet. The directions are easy to follow and require very little in the way of culinary skills. And soon, I'm bringing her a steaming bowl of soup and crackers.

Her appetite isn't there yet. She stirs the soup, but hasn't committed to eating anything yet. Part of me wants to call Fletcher because he's going to be pissed if anything happens to her. But loyalty wins out.

"I won't call him if you eat something."

Her eyes narrow, but she knows defeat. "Fine, but tell me. What's going on with you? I feel like a dick I haven't called you back, but I can barely keep my eyes open these days."

"You mean, when your eyes are open, they are busy giving Fletcher those come hither looks. That's how you got knocked up."

I miss my friend like crazy, but I can't be mad at her for living the life she's always dreamed. She has the career and guy she's always wanted. And she's always taken care of everyone, including her ex and me until he crossed over into crazy town.

"I found out who my mom is," I announce.

The spoon that had been halfway to her lips slips from her hand and causes soup to splatter all over the tray.

"What? Why didn't you call me?"

I don't have to answer as she realizes that I had called her. "Damn, Gina. I'm so sorry."

Shaking my head, I say, "It's okay. You were busy."

"Never too busy for you. I swear, it's been crazy traveling back and forth, taking care of patients and trying to keep an eye on my dad."

"Exactly. And I love you for that. I'm good—really."

She sighs with pain and regret so obvious in her face. She leans over and wraps me in a hug. And that's when I finally loose my shit. I'd been holding it in all this time, but my birth mom had contacted me, and that was a big fucking deal.

I'm a torrent of emotions. "She wants to meet me," I begin before I tell her the rest of it.

Before I leave, she's tucked in bed. We both have answers about what to do next. I promise to spend the night at her house, not wanting to leave her alone. I talk to Sam about getting the day off when I go into the bar that night and get the green light.

All my plans change a few days later when I get the call. I hadn't had much communication with Ryder because he had games and practice. We'd traded sexy texts, but I hadn't seen him. Tonight, I'm supposed to show up at his game wearing his jersey, and that's not going to happen.

"I'll go with you," Mark says.

He's at my house because we were planning to ride to the game together. I nod and send off a text to Ryder he probably won't see until after the game.

Me: I'm sorry I couldn't make it tonight. I'll explain when I see you.

There is so much I want to tell him, but I want to do it in person.

On the private plane that has been arranged, Mark looks as lost as I feel.

"Tell me what you're thinking?" I ask.

The setting sunlight shoots through the window and highlights just how handsome Mark is. The woman who snags him will be the lucky one.

"Are you sure about this?"

I shrug. "Do I have a choice?"

"Have you told your boyfriend?"

"He has a name."

"He does, but can you call him your boyfriend?"

I shift to look anywhere, but at him.

"Gina, you know I love you. I've loved you since third grade probably. And Ryder's a good guy. Don't let your fear ruin things."

Bluster and deflection, my main go-tos shape my tongue.

"What is that supposed to mean?"

There is a long moment.

"It means when anyone gets too close, you shut them out unless they are checked safely in your friend box."

As he said it, he held my gaze. But as soon as the words leave his mouth, he can't look at me. And I hate I'd hurt him so long ago. But he's right. It's easier to let someone go first before they have a chance to hurt you.

"I love you, Mark."

Sad eyes briefly glance at me. "I know you do, and you deserve someone who is going to make you his fairy princess."

His use of Ryder's term for me causes a lump to form in my throat.

Whispering, I say, "What if—"

He cuts me off, "You'll never know unless you try."

"What about you? That girl you wouldn't tell me about before."

"Apparently, she's not interested in dating jobless guys." He shrugs and then he squares his shoulders with a twinkle in his eye. "Who knows, maybe I'll get another shot with Riley."

My jaw drops and finally his face fills with mirth.

"Spill," I say, remembering when his name was mentioned before I thought I caught a sign of recognition she hadn't copped to.

RYDER

Every chance I get, I find myself scanning the stands, searching for Gina. But no success. My stupid imagination is filled with images of her wearing my jersey, along with the Cougars hat, cheering me on. Disappointment ends up being the name of my game as far as that goes. The pitching coach has me step in as a reliever in the bottom of the fifth. Forcing every thought of that black-haired sex engine out of my mind, by some miracle, I end up pitching the game of my life. The manager leaves me in until the ninth inning when I'm replaced by the closer. I've given up zero runs and only one batter gets a hit off me. Maybe it was anger that fueled my arm, but whatever. The congratulatory pats on my back feel good, but do little to replace what I would've felt if Gina had lived up to her agreement to be here.

We end up with a solid win, which puts us one step closer to the playoffs. When I get to the locker room, I grab my phone and see Gina's text. If that's supposed to make me feel better, it's an epic fail. In fact, it pisses me off even more. She waited until the last possible minute to send it, knowing I wouldn't get it until after the game. What the fuck is that all about? Does she have such little respect for me that she can't even give me an explanation of any kind?

Sorry, Ryder, but I couldn't make it because I had to wash my hair. Or, *Sorry, Ryder, I needed to go out and buy some toothpaste, so I hate that I missed the most important game of your career.*

All this shit rolls through my head while I shower and sours my mood, even after the accolades on our win.

As I'm packing up my duffle bag and getting ready to leave, Robinson yells, "Hey, Ryder, you coming?"

"What?"

"You coming with us? You know, to celebrate?"

"Oh." I scratch my chin. "I don't know. I'm wiped out."

"Yeah, but you need to party, dude. You totally killed it out there."

"Thanks, man. Appreciate it."

He grabs my arm and starts pulling me in the direction of the exit. "I'm not taking no for an answer. Let's get out of here."

Looks like I won't be getting out of this, so I follow him to The Cougars Beer Stand, the team's favorite watering hole. The place is jammed when we get there. The management is even present, including Ms.

Whitestone herself. She's buying drinks for everyone, and it appears it's going to be party time tonight. I might as well join in the fun.

"Ryder, that was one hell of a game you threw tonight."

"Thanks, Ms. Whitestone."

"One step closer to that ace position you covet so much."

I shrug. I think it's bad karma to talk about this in front of other players, so my deal is to play it off as noncommittal. But she doesn't drop it.

"I owe you a favor anyway, for what you did for me. You know, the escort service?"

Heads turn our way when she mentions it.

Immediately, I jump in with, "How could I forget? It's a great charity. I love kids, and I was glad to help raise money for such a worthy cause." Hopefully, that will stop the gossipers from starting any crazy rumors.

A shot of something clear is shoved in my hand, and everyone around us raises their glasses as we toast our win. I down the clear stuff, and it burns a path to my stomach. Someone calls my name and motions me over. It's the perfect distraction, so I excuse myself and head in that direction. Another shot of something, this time it's red, is handed to me. I honestly don't want it, but if I don't down it, they'll call me a pussy. That's one moniker I don't want attached to my name. So I tip the glass, and in one long swallow, it's down the hatch. It's sweet and leaves my mouth feeling sticky, so I know to stay away from that crap.

Pushing my way through the crowd, I make it up to the bar and order a Jameson on the rocks. It reminds me of my cousin, Fletcher, and that I need to give him a call. His season is underway, and the Rockets are having a helluva year so far.

"Hey, Ryder. Great game, man." It's one of the other pitchers, and he slaps me on the back.

"Thanks. I appreciate that. Great work in closing out the game."

He nods. "Hey, keep that up and you'll be the starter next season."

"Oh, I don't know about that."

"Your speed, accuracy, and the fact that you've never been injured or have had any issues make you a pretty good bet." He acts damn convincing. "But, cheers. Here's to a great game."

We clink glasses. With the way the alcohol is flowing, it won't take long for me to get tanked. The music is loud, and people are already dancing.

All of a sudden, one of the guys yells out, "Tequila shots on the house."

David Lester moves in on the other side of me and says, "My fucking head is going to be exploding all over town tomorrow."

"Same here."

Then I see one of our outfielders walking by guzzling a bottle of champagne. I hope no one plans on driving.

David leans close to my ear and says, "What do you

think about Whitestone?"

"What do you mean?" I ask.

"Would you fuck her? She's a pretty hot cougar, if you ask me. You know, cougars and MILFs are the thing these days."

"Lester, who are you? Are you the same guy who wanted to tour a corn pipe factory in Ashville and had never been to a sex club?"

David laughs and ignores my jab. "What? She remind you too much of Mom?"

"Okay, that's just disgusting. You can't be saying shit like that, man."

All I can see is Gina with her dark hair, smooth as silk skin, and gorgeous eyes, and I say, "I think I'll pass on that one." The thought almost makes me gag.

"Yeah, sorry." He shakes his head, still chuckling.

"Besides, it's not that—"

He doesn't give me a chance to finish. "That's right. You're with someone, that girl from the club, aren't you?"

"Thought I was," is all I say.

"You two break it off?" David asks.

"I don't know what the fuck we are, if you want the truth."

A waitress walks by with those test tube shots, and David buys a couple. "Here." He hands me one. "You need one of these."

I down it, and it tastes like butterscotch. I have no idea what I'm drinking, but I don't even care anymore. "I

142

don't think I need any more alcohol." My words are already slurred.

"Who does?" he asks. "The point isn't that we *need* it. It's that we *want* it, Wilde."

As I glance across the room, it suddenly looks like a swarm of half-naked women have invaded this place. Their phones are out as they snap pictures of everyone.

"Photo alert. The groupies have descended," I say.

David turns around as three of them approach us.

"Aren't you Ryder Wilde?" one of them asks.

David points at me and says, "That's him. In the flesh."

One of them, a bleached blond says, "Oooh, can I get a picture with you?"

Not giving me a chance to reply, she sidles next to me and takes a selfie. I'm sure I appear to be a wide-eyed inebriated idiot. The other two replace her and do the same. Then all three of them are hunkered around me, and I am the object of the selfie invasion. More women approach me, and I see David backing away, laughing. That fucker. They grab my ass, my arms, my pecs, and one of them even does a crotch squeeze and tries to massage my balls. What the hell kind of women are these?

"We heard you like it wild, Mr. Wilde."

"Yeah, well, you heard wrong. I'm the tame sort, if you want to know the truth." By now, the vultures have me backed against the bar, and I'm trapped, with no escape in sight. One of them leans into my face, and she smells like week old stale beer. Short of decking them with my fists, I don't know what the hell to do.

But then I hear, "Excuse me, ladies. I need to have a little chat with Mr. Wilde."

The crowd parts like the Red Sea, and there stands Whitestone in all her cougar glory. And I have never been so happy to see anyone in my life. I nearly throw myself at her fuck me pumps.

She grabs my hand, and I hold on to it like the lifeline from a rescue boat as we sail on past the groupies. We get to a place where the crowd has thinned, and I get ready to thank her. Before I can utter a single syllable, her mouth crashes onto mine, and I am stupefied as she proceeds to kiss me. The only thing I can think of is at least she doesn't smell like week old stale beer. But then it hits me, despite the shadowy corner she pulls me into, I realize there are people around us, watching.

Fuck!

Placing my hands on her upper arms, I move her to a safe distance away, and her sly grin tells me more than I need to know.

"Ryder, come home with me. It will be worth your while in more ways than what you're thinking."

Even in my drunken state, I know what I need to do. "I'm flattered, Ms. Whitestone, but I'm seriously involved in a relationship."

She pouts, "That's too bad." But that only lasts for a second. Then her red-stained lips curve upward. "Are you sure about that?"

"I'm sure."

"You're passing up an opportunity of a lifetime."

Having a one-night stand with a woman my mother's age doesn't seem so to me, but I keep the smile pasted on my face. "I'm glad you think so highly of me, but I have to say no." And I almost add—thanks for thinking of me—but change my mind at the last minute. It's a good thing. That would've sounded stupid, exactly how I feel right now.

She pats my cheek, and her thumb swipes lipstick from my mouth. Out of the corner of my eye I see people with their phones out snapping pictures. Great. Just great. Now everyone is going to think we're an item. Fuck me backwards. And upside down while you're at it. This is all I need. If Gina catches wind of this, she's never going to believe I was innocent. But then again, do I really care? She's the one who stood me up today.

I stand there and watch Ms. Whitestone walk away and wonder where the fuck Gina is anyway. And that thought brings in the pissed off as hell feeling all over again. So, what do I do? I head back to the bar for another tequila shot. The way I figure is what the fuck. I may as well drown my Gina sorrows now, because I'm sure I'll be paying for it later.

GINA

The plane ride should have been enjoyable. Instead, I'm a nervous wreck. How can I not be? Thank goodness for Mark. His presence calms my nerves. I spend half the time on the phone with Cassie and the other being consoled by Mark. Between the two of them, they prepare me for what I'm about to face.

Now I stand in front of a door at a house that isn't mine. Mark's earlier hug and encouragement have helped me get to this point because he hasn't been allowed to accompany me. I take a deep breath and turn the handle.

I don't know what to expect. As I walk into a well-lit large room with many windows and furniture of museum quality, I see what may be a mirror into my future. The woman in the bed with a duvet tucked to her waist leans against the headboard wearing glasses on a face that looks more like me than I dreamed. She also doesn't look as frail as I expected. My emotions are raw and all over the place.

"Gina." Her voice is as regal as the house. I glance up from the spot on the floor I'd found a second before. "I never did like that name."

Snarky me is quick with a response. "I guess you shouldn't have given me up then."

My words are sharp, but the contempt I feel cannot be contained.

"So much like your father."

I release a humorless laugh. "Not sure why you would think that. You barely knew the man, and he barely knows me. He was too busy living his own life to be bothered with a child he didn't want."

She slides off her glasses, and I'm more surprised by her unlined face. Then again, with the money this woman has, I shouldn't have expected less. In fact, her hair is darker than mine with no hint of her true age.

"That's unfortunate," she says.

"You know what's unfortunate? That I'm here. I've been led to believe that you are on your deathbed. But I assume now that was a lie to get me here."

"Gina."

I hold up a hand.

"Please, don't bother. I missed my boyfriend's game for this lie of yours. And just so you know, I don't want your money or your lifestyle. Obviously, you are a very lonely woman to pull a trick to get me here."

Spinning on my heels, I march toward the door when

she says so calmly, "Boyfriend. That wouldn't be Ryder Wilde? Apparently, he doesn't know the meaning of a relationship if the pictures of him in the tabloids are to be believed."

Slowly, I turn to face her. "That's low, even for you. You don't know him."

Anger wells up inside me. I trust him. I do.

A pale wrist lifts with a remote clutched in it. A tap on the iPad on her lap and the TV behind me comes to life. I turn to see a reporter, if you can call her that, fill the screen.

"Pictures of Ryder Wilde have surfaced all over the internet and social media. After his spectacular win that clenched the Cougars into the playoffs, he was seen with not one but three women. That isn't what caught our eyes. It was the pictures of him lip-locked with the owner of the Cougars that have us all wondering what's going on with the up and coming pitcher and the owner of the team."

I have no idea the depths of my feelings for the man until tears form in my eyes, but I hold them at bay. Instead, I swallow my pride and face the woman who gave me half of my DNA.

Shrugging, I say, "We have an open relationship."

The lie is blatant, but I said it anyway to save face.

A perfectly polished nail strikes the iPad, silencing the room.

"Is that so? Is that why you haven't ended your membership to that sex club?"

Slack-jawed, I open and close my mouth a few times before I say, "You've been checking up on me."

Her skin pales, and a sheen of sweat forms on her stately face. She wheezes out her next word, "Yes."

That's when I get something is wrong. The façade she's made crumbles. Still, I ask the question. "Why?"

She reaches under her pillow and pulls out what appears to be an inhaler. She sucks in a deep breath from the object and exhales long.

A few seconds later, she glances up at me. She labors through as she speaks. "I know you might not believe me, but if I had been as strong as you, I would not have given you up. Since I have had control of the company, I have done my best to make sure you were okay. I had a private detective check up on you. The pictures he brought back were of a well-adjusted teen. If I had known..."

"Well-adjusted." I laugh. "I did what I had to do. It's not like Dad beat me or anything. He just wasn't there."

"Your grandparents?" she croaks.

"They raised their son." I figure that is as good enough answer.

"I'm sorry," she whispers.

"Yeah, me, too."

Then we stare at one another. I fidget, not sure what to do at this point because a part of me believes her or wants to. The other part is still mad for the life I never had.

She struggles to speak, and her voice has lost its

149

bravado. "The company and everything you see and everything that is mine is still yours. It will be deeded to you. It will be simpler if you just sign the documents now and avoid probate."

My cold heart starts to melt because I can see that she is as sick as I was led to believe. Still, where was she when I needed a mom?

"Is there someone I can call to help you?"

Shaking her head, she lifts the other hand and presses a button on a cylindrical object. Not two seconds later, a team of people swarm into the room like bees buzzing about. An oxygen mask is placed over her face, and a young woman with a stern expression, probably due to the severe bun at the nape of her neck, corrals me over to the side.

"Ms. Vecchio needs her rest. She has instructed me to offer you a room to stay for the night."

Immediately, I shake my head no. The woman, who has yet to introduce herself, glances back at my birth mom. Silent communication happens, and I can tell this woman has been in her employ for some time.

"She suspected as much and rooms have been booked at a hotel for you and your companion."

Companion? I don't bother to correct her. The less these people know about me the better. It feels as though I have few secrets left if she's been checking into my life. And for how long?

"I would like to go home."

The woman places her hand on my arm. "She

doesn't have a lot of time. If I were you, I would consider that this may be your last time you'll be able to talk with her."

As overwhelmed as I am, she's right. Are there questions I have? I'm not sure. But maybe sleeping on it before running will be a good idea. I nod my head.

I give the bed and my mother one last glance before I'm ushered out of the room.

Later, I pace the hotel room, confused about everything. So many times I've typed a message to Ryder, only to erase it. I stop, knowing Mark is waiting for me downstairs. We are to have drinks down at the bar. So finally, I decide on the truth.

Me: I'm sorry I missed your game. I wasn't given a lot of time when I was told to come meet my birth mother before she passed on. But it looks like you made the best of your win. Congratulations.

It's a long message, but says everything that needed saying. Childishly, I turn off my phone and head to the bar where Mark and I drink until closing and find our way back to our rooms.

The next morning, I wake with heavy eyes and blurred vision. The pounding in my head is like a bass drum on steroids. I need coffee like fish need water. The suite at the five-star hotel has a full kitchen, and I make my way there.

Before I can get the coffee started, I hear heated voices outside my door. I press at the pressure points on my temple and make my way for the door. Opening it, I find Ryder and the lawyer locked like stags over the last doe.

"Ryder, why are you here? And how did you find me?"

He flashes me a smile that gets me wet. Damn him.

"My cousin is Fletcher," he announces proudly.

There is no need to explain more. Traitors, the both of them, Cassie and Mark have turned to the dark side no doubt. But I'll have words with them both.

Ryder scoots by Mr. Giovanni like he owns the place. The other man scowls.

"Your mother would like to see you this morning," the lawyer says.

I nod. "Give me five."

Then I close the door in the lawyer's face. Crossing my arms over my chest, I pivot and face the man who's starred in every dream I've had since I met him for the first time.

"Shouldn't you be fucking your way to the ace position?"

That dulls the beautiful smile from his face.

"Got your claws out this morning, I see."

I shrug, hoping he can't see the hurt that hides just below the surface of my skin.

"That's what you think of me."

"I don't know. It's hard to discount your lips on hers."

"Her lips on mine, you mean. I didn't see it coming."

I let out a harrumph. "I'll give you that one. But what

about the girl with her hands on your dick?"

"Jesus, Gina. I didn't ask for any of it. It isn't like I can fight back."

I turn around because seeing him makes it hard for me to say what I have to say next.

"And this is why I can't be your girlfriend. I have trust issues. I'm not built for relationships."

"I guess not. You couldn't bother to tell me the truth."

Whirling around, I say, "I didn't think it was a good idea to dump my problems on you before your game. Excuse me for being considerate."

"Yeah, and how long have you known about your long-lost mother?"

Pursing my lips, I say nothing because he has me there.

"And, I see you brought Mark with you. He knows more about your life than I do. Maybe you should be dating him."

His hurled words sting like a slap.

"Mark doesn't have a job and could travel with me. I didn't exactly ask him to come. He insisted."

I brush back my hair, feeling uncomfortable with the way the conversation is going. My bluster breaks because it fucking kills me knowing that this will end with him walking away.

"And you can't see he's still in love with you."

I snap my attention in his direction and narrow my eyes at him. "You are so wrong. I think he's got a thing for your sister." After saying it, I clamp my hand over my mouth, knowing I've blown a secret that wasn't mine to share. "Don't you dare open your filthy mouth and tell her."

He licks his lips. "And what will you do for me to keep my filthy mouth shut?"

RYDER

The challenge has been tossed, but what will she do? Will this play into my hands, like I hope it will? Or will Gina turn and run, as she's used to doing?

Her breathing changes, and her eyes go wicked with all the possibilities. "What's it gonna take, Cowboy?"

Half-smiling, I shrug. "Oh, I don't know. Why don't you come up with something?" My parents used to do this to me as a kid. They would make me come up with my own punishment when I did something wrong. Since I'm scared shitless she's ready to take a hike, I decide to use their tactic.

Her fingers pick up a chunk of hair and twirl it as she thinks. Her bottom lip pulls in, the same one I want to suck, or she can use that mouth to suck on me. Then those gorgeous eyes squint at me. Still soft from sleeping, all I want to do is pull her against me and run my hands over her silky skin. Only wearing a cami and tiny boxers, she's a wet dream with her bed hair and heavy lidded eyes.

Pounding on the door interrupts us. "Gina, we have

to go. We are on a schedule, as there isn't a lot of time left." It's that damn man who tried to bar me from entering.

"I have to go. As my text message said, my birth mother is on her deathbed. That's why I had to fly here. It could be any time now."

"Gina, I—"

"Please, can we talk about this later? I need to get ready."

"Yeah, sure." I glance at the door. Mark and the lawyer asshole are out there talking, so I opt to stay where I am.

She pulls off her cami, heading to the bedroom, and I consider tossing her on the bed and fucking both of us senseless.

"If you stay in here, Cowboy, I fear neither one of us will leave this room." She closes the door so she can get dressed. I know she's right, even if I don't like it. Another knock sounds on the door.

I let the asshole in the suite, and Mark follows.

"Hey, what gives?" I ask the snake that wants my girl. "I'm tired of his ridiculous attitude toward me."

"Ms. Ferraro has a lot to attend to and doesn't need any distractions today," he says.

"I get that. You don't have to worry. We keep our distractions behind closed doors." Mark snickers, the ass grimaces, and I manage not to smile. "I'll go with her so I can be of assistance."

"That won't be necessary. I am her mother's

attorney and can assist her in every way."

What the fuck does that mean?

"Is that right?"

He acts more arrogant than anyone I've ever met. "Yes, that's right. In fact, you should leave. Ms. Ferraro has no need for you here at all."

"Wait," Mark says with a raised hand. "I think Gina needs to be the judge of that."

"What do I need to be the judge of?" Gina asks as she comes out of the bedroom.

"Mr. Fancy Pants here just told me to leave and that you have no need for me. That he will be the one assisting you in every way." My fists clench at my sides. I wait for Gina's response. Her mouth opens and closes, and I know she doesn't know what to say, which is unusual for her.

She finally asks me, "When do you have to be back?"

"I'm off for three days."

Then she holds out her hand and says, "Will you come with me? I really want you to." I place my calloused hand in her soft one, and she grips it with a strength that surprises me.

What's even better is when she turns to Mr. Fancy Pants and says, "Let me be clear. You work for my mother. And I'm not a child. I decide who will assist me in every way. Are we clear?"

I watch him back down and swallow whatever he might have said. "Yes, Ms. Ferraro, but I work for you, too."

Then Gina looks at Mark and says, "Come on, too. We might as well make this a party. I'll need all the support I can get to muddle through this." He falls in line behind us as we make our way to the fancy limo that awaits us.

On the ride there, Gina never releases her hold of my hand. I'm happy to be her rock, her support, her I-beam—whatever the hell she needs. Damn, I'll carry the woman on my back if I have to.

Her mother's house is a sprawling estate by the water, but the only people around are the help. It's weird because there is no family here to support her in her final days. I don't ask, and I'm not even sure if Gina would know. My role is to be here for my girl, and I am. But Gina's sadness, though we don't talk about it, is I think that she never knew the woman who lies dying. It's the oddest thing, too. My family is tight. It's unimaginable for me to think of not knowing my mother, so seeing Gina with this near stranger really tugs at my heartstrings. Everything tumbles into place now why she keeps pushing me away, why she doesn't want a relationship, why she's afraid. It seems to me her fears are grounded. If her mother never had the time to get to know her, to discover what a beautiful person she is, then why would anyone else?

When the crowd around her bed finally disperses, the woman motions to Gina to come closer. I figure she'd want to go alone, but she doesn't release my hand, so I tag along.

Her mother lifts up her oxygen mask and wheezes, "Ryder Wilde, I presume?"

"Yes, ma'am," I say.

"Manners." She coughs into a cloth.

It's very awkward standing here, and I'm not sure if I should say anything. *Nice to meet you* seems a bit lame.

But then she almost scolds Gina by saying, "Introduce us."

"Oh, M-mother, this is Ryder. Ryder, this is Ms. Vecchio."

"Nice to meet you, ma'am."

She sucks in a deep breath and manages to wheeze out a long string of words.

"It is not. You look like you're about ready to squirm, standing there. There's nothing nice about meeting a dying woman for the first time. But I am glad you came here with my Gina. Now, please tell her to go with my attorney and sign the damn papers before I die." She plunks her oxygen mask back down over her face.

Pulling Gina's hand, she faces me. "Papers?"

"Yeah, she wants to sign everything over to me."

Ms. Vecchio pulls off her mask again. "She's getting it whether or not she wants it, now or after I die. If she signs now, it'll avoid probate."

I turn back to her and take her hands in mine.

"Trust me, Gina. Sign the damn papers. You do not want the probate headache."

Her eyes search mine. Clearly, she's lost.

"Hang on a sec." I leave the room and get Mark. He's

159

quite a strong influence on her, and knowing Gina, she's not shared any of this with him. I locate him downstairs, lying on a couch in one of the many rooms.

"Hey, I need you." I explain the situation.

"She never said a word about this." Mark runs a hand through his already bedhead.

"I figured as much."

"Christ, she doesn't have a clue what a damn mess this would be. Let's go."

Gina stands by the bed as we both enter the room. It's clear the two had words, and Gina appears shaken while the woman in the bed looks like she aged a decade in the few minutes I've been gone. Mark drags her to the side, and we all have a serious conversation about this.

"I don't want her company," she declares adamantly.

"You're getting it whether you want it or not. Trust me on this. What you *don't* want is probate. Sign the fucking papers. I doubt she ran everything. There will be people to do that for you." Mark's hand is on her arm, and he's not letting her get out of this.

"Listen to him, Gina. If you think it's bad now, let this slide and you'll be in a fucking wasp's nest."

Her sigh is heavy, but I can tell our double teaming worked. "Okay, okay. Where are they?"

I walk into the hall to hunt down Mr. Fancy Pants. When I find him, I put him to work.

Within a matter of thirty minutes, everything is signed and sealed. Gina is now a very wealthy woman, I surmise.

Gina and her mom spend more time together alone. Mark and I are treated like kings by the wait staff. We catch Fletcher and Cassie up on the latest, and they promise to fly into town as soon as they can.

Before I have to head back to report to practice and to get ready for my next game, her mother passes. Gina tries to hide her distress, but it's plain on her face. Clearly, the woman had been waiting to meet her daughter and take care of things so she could leave this world. But at least they had a few days to hash things out.

When we get back to the hotel, Mark brings up a bottle of vodka and some wine from the bar downstairs, along with some mixers. We make some drinks, and I want to know how Gina is feeling.

"It's so odd, but I'm much sadder than I thought I would be," she says.

"You just lost your mother," Mark says.

She rubs her face and answers, "But I only met her for the first time a few days ago. It's not like I knew her."

Grabbing her arm, I pull her onto my lap, and the resistance I expect never comes. "It's probably because you saw what could've been, and that's what's making you sad."

"Yeah, maybe. My dad had that whole parade of women going and I never had a mom, so I guess it's regret and sadness all tied up with a pretty bow. Then all these images I had of her were blown away because she was nothing like I'd imagined. I wish I had met her earlier. And worse, she left me journals and pictures."

Both our phones start buzzing. When we check them, we laugh. Hers is Cassie, and mine is Fletcher calling.

After we update them, they want to know if they should fly out. Gina assures them she's fine, and the funeral is going to be held in two days. It will be private, so there's no need.

That night, Gina pulls me into bed, but before I can even put my lips on hers, she's softly snoring next to me. As I curl my body around hers, I wonder what's in store for our future. Will she want to stay here and live in her mother's home? Will she want to take the reins of her mom's empire? Now that she's the head of it, her mind may change. All this can spell a significant alteration for our relationship. Long distances don't bode well for them, and with her trust issues, I can see how this could work against us. It kills because I don't think I want to live without this woman in my life, but it may be that I don't have a choice.

GINA

Waking up back at home, I feel safe in Ryder's arms. He's like a comfortable blanket wrapped all around me, and I hate I have to leave his safety. It's still dark when I creep out of the bed, his breathing soft and steady. Before leaving my room, I unzip the small overnight bag I took and pull out the leather bound portfolio.

Sitting on my couch, I curl up in the corner as I undo the ties that hold everything together. Once open, I think about everything my mother told me in the short time we shared before she passed on.

The first picture to tumble free is me on my first day of school. I remember being so scared. I didn't remember the picture or that I'd been missing a tooth. But as my mother explained, it was part of a side agreement for my grandparents to send her pictures of me. Something her father was unaware of, as he'd been the reason she had to give me up or be disowned.

But that isn't the most shocking thing she told me over the course of a few days. Over the last several years, even when I was still in high school, she'd reached out to my father. Her parents had passed on by then, and she was free to make her own decisions without consequences.

My parents, who shared one summer together, became confidants of each other at some point. And recently, when she told him of her illness, he admitted truths she hadn't known. Not surprisingly, he was put out when she showed up and announced he was a father. He hadn't wanted his life to change. In the end, though, he told her he regretted not being the father I needed. I look at a picture taken of me at one of my softball games. She told me Dad secretly came to my games, but kept to the shadows, not feeling he deserved seeing me play, but unable to stay away.

I wipe hateful tears that spill from my cheeks as I think of the biggest revelation. Dad had told her how proud he was of me to be the woman I am despite the lack of parental guidance in my life.

My world is shaken and stirred. Everything I thought isn't as it seemed. Dad isn't the uncaring father that I thought he was. My mother did love me just not enough. And Ryder…

Warm hands slide down my arms.

"Hey, fairy princess. Why are you up?" His words fan across my neck.

I lean my head back, exposing myself in a way I never

have before. His hands leave my arms and begin to wipe the tears from my face. Then he plants a kiss movie-worthy style on my lips.

"Don't cry," he says, which only makes me cry harder.

Then he frees my hands of my bundle. He sets it on the coffee table before lifting me onto his lap after he takes a seat. I bury my face in his chest as he rubs circles on my back, and I ugly cry until no more tears will come.

"Ryder," I croak, pulling free somewhat of his embrace.

"Yes." His word is soft and full of something more than *like* that I'd always been afraid of; that other four letter L word.

"Thank you."

"You don't have to thank me."

"Yes... Yes, I do. I've been so selfish. You've done so many things for me. I don't know why you put up with me. It would have been so easy for you to walk away, yet you didn't."

He touches my nose, then my check, then brushes his fingers over my lips.

"I don't give up so easily when I see a good thing."

"A good thing," I repeat, not feeling worthy of that title.

"Yes, a good thing. Whether you want to believe it or not, I see you. And I've seen you through Fletcher. I've seen you with Cassie, and even Mark. What guy wants to be friends with his ex?" His brow lifts, daring me to contradict that statement. "Exactly. No guy unless said girl is so very worth it. I just wanted to show you how worth it you are."

"It's not just the sex?" I ask, my self-esteem on the floor for him to walk all over.

"The sex?" He chuckles. "If anything, sex with you should have had me running for the hills."

Playfully, I slap him, but a part of me is stung by his words. I thought we'd crossed that barrier. He'd given me his hard limit, and I'd agreed. And more and more, I found just being with him was enough. I hadn't even made any requests I've made of other lovers. Now worry fills me.

He flinches from my love tap, but laughs. "No, seriously. Sex with you is an adventure."

I eye him, waiting for the other shoe to fall.

"In a good way. Can't you feel exactly how much I want you? I'm trying to be a gentleman here and talk to you, but I can show you just how much I've missed being inside you these last few days."

He hadn't pressed for it the nights we'd come back from me seeing her, me emotionally drained knowing her end was near. There are so many reasons I should kiss him and get to the good part. However, there are things that need to be said.

"This thing with my mom and her business," I move my head slowly side to side, "I don't know where that leads me."

"You haven't told me. What kind of business did you

inherit?"

The lawyer refused to explain all of that in front of the guys. Confidentiality and all of that. But I'm in charge now.

"It's a conglomerate whose headquarters are currently run out of Italy." Though my mother lived in the States, so I don't think I have to move. "They own mines of gold and gems, companies that make fine jewelry and fashion houses of some well-known designer brands. All of which is completely out of my element."

Ryder, ever my champion, makes me feel smart by his sheer confidence in me.

"You have a head for business. I see how you manage the bar when Sam is in the back taking care of other things."

"That's the bar. And I'm not sure I can be Cassie or a future mom. I love her to death, but I feel restless. A part of me wants to run. I want to see the world and find myself."

He stares at me with the most beautiful eyes, and I begin to waver on my resolve.

"What are you saying?"

"I'm saying, trust doesn't come easy to me, and neither does love. I don't know how to be a girlfriend. And you've seen how I've messed that up epically. I'm not sure what I want to do with my life now. There are so many possibilities."

"You don't know how you feel about me?" he asks, sounding confused and maybe a little hurt.

"I know exactly how I feel about you. I'm falling in love with you, if I'm not there already, and it scares the ever living shit out of me."

"But that's—"

I cut him off with a finger to his lips. "Don't say it. I need time. And it's not fair for me to hold you back. I'll only be a distraction when you are headed to the playoffs."

"Gina…" he breathes.

"Make love to me, Ryder. One last time."

He stares at me as I plead with unspoken words. And then he does. I crash my lips against his and slip my hand beneath his waistband to quiet his protest. I free us from our clothes as we use our lips, tongues, hands, and fingers to bring us to epic orgasms. We fall asleep, but when I wake, I pack a small bag and leave. The note I leave on the table says *I'm sorry* and *I love you* in the same breath. It also says *don't wait for me*. That's the hardest thing to do. I don't have the balls to say it to his face because he'll only convince me we can do this together. This, however, is a journey I need to make alone.

Dawn has barely passed when I roll up to my father's house. Luckily, his wife, or whatever she is, sleeps late, but I know Dad to be a morning bird.

He sits on the steps of the porch as if he knew I was coming.

"Dad," I say, setting the kickstand on the bike and hoping my arrival didn't wake the wicked witch.

Being back on my Harley steadied me for the conversation to come.

"Gina." He gives me a two finger salute. "I guess you're here to tell me she's gone."

I nod, and he nods back, firing up a cigarette—a nasty habit he hasn't been able to kick. I sit, and he blows a stream of noxious fumes in the opposite direction.

"She told you, huh," he says.

The fact that he reads my showing up so well makes perfect sense with everything my absent mother was able to tell me about the father I'd grown up with. *The irony.*

"Why didn't you come to me? We could have worked things out."

"Gina, you were well set in your dislike of me, not that I blame you."

He's right on that score. I doubt if I would have believed anything he said. Having it come from a perfect stranger made it easier for me to accept.

He adds, "What did you think of her?"

I'm not really sure. Part of me hates her, and part of me understands. "I get she didn't have a choice but to give me up. What would she have done at seventeen with a kid and no job and no place to go? Where would my life be now? At the same time, she wasn't seventeen forever. Where was she the rest of my twenty-seven years? Not like it matters. How can I hate her now? She's dead."

Dad's quiet for a little bit. "She loved you."

"I got that."

"And I did, too, though I was too selfish and too stupid to show it. And I'm sorry for it."

I blink back tears. So many things I've longed to hear. Is it too late? I switch subjects.

"What did you do with your share of the money?"

He sucks in hard on his cancer stick and blows out smoke rings, which used to fascinate me as a child. "Got a vasectomy. It took some convincing to the doctors because I was young, but I got it done. You showing up scared the shit out of me, and I didn't want that surprise again."

Not a selfish choice totally if one takes the time to think it through. He could have blown it on something stupid. His decision took his future into account and maybe even a little of my own.

"Any regrets?" I ask.

He shakes his head as I watch the burning embers at the end of his cigarette.

"But that didn't use all the money," he confesses.

I could have responded, but I let him decide what he wants to tell me.

"Mom and Dad did use most of the money on you and fixing up your room and shit. I don't want you to think they saw you as a paycheck or nothing."

Biting my tongue, I don't correct his grammar. The little girl in me wants to believe him and see him as my silent hero, nothing else. So I don't ask exactly how much money had been given to them. My mother hadn't offered that detail either.

"You don't have to tell me," I say.

He points straight ahead with the cigarette in his hand. "I got you that bike."

"What do you mean..." I protest, but my words trail off.

I'd wanted a bike. Something about riding on one after one of my dates had made me feel alive, so I'd inquired around to buy one. I'd even gone so far as to ask my dad if he knew of someone selling a used one. I'd saved, but working jobs here and there didn't make for buying a new or used Harley at that time.

"You didn't go to college, and I've got to believe that was my fault for not encouraging you. And you wanted a bike. I had the money. I figured one day I'd give you the money for school. You remember I even asked if you were going. You said no, so I talked to Billy and he found you a bike. I paid for most of it and had him tell you some poor chap wanted to get rid of it for a song and a prayer."

I thought it was my lucky day that I'd asked at the right time to the right people.

"I didn't know," I whisper.

"I know."

"And you let me think the worst of you."

His cheeks hollow as he pulls in toxic air. I want to knock the damn thing from his hand now that I have my father. I don't want him to die from some form of cancer just when I think we can find some common ground.

"Hey, Tig. What you doin' out here?" The voice comes from a silhouette at the door.

Damn, the witch was up. And that nickname of his. Most women called my dad, Tiger, and I shudder to think why.

"Talkin' to my daughter."

"What's she doin' here?" The cruelty in her voice is crippling.

That's my cue to leave because the last thing I want is for the good talk I had with my dad to end in a shouting match with the evil witch. I start to get to my feet, but my father's hand lands on my shoulder and holds me in place.

"She's my daughter, and she's welcome any time. If you got a problem with that, you can pack your shit and go."

Damn, if he didn't make me want to clap. For the first time ever, he stands up to her. And my father hasn't been one to let a woman walk over him until her.

I watch with a grin as she backs up and scuttles away without another word. She's probably flabbergasted he talked to her that way.

"I should be going anyway," I say.

"Just one more thing."

"What's that?"

"I don't want any of her money. That's for you. Don't try to give me none either."

I could tell him that his use of double negatives

cancels each other out, and in actuality he's telling me to give him the money. But I know what he means, which takes me for a loop. Part of me wonders if his change of heart has something to do with the number of zeros in my bank account.

"What do you want?" I ask.

Blowing out a final stream of smoke, he tosses the remnant on the ground and uses his boot to squash the thing to death.

"I want a chance to really get to know you."

Standing, he holds out a hand. Dumbly, I nod and then I'm enveloped in his tall frame.

"I like Ryder by the way."

Pulling out of his embrace, my jaw flaps open, and I'm greeted with a huge smile.

As I ride the highway out of town so I can let loose and really let the wind whip through my hair, I think about that conversation. I think about Ryder. I think about the mother I won't ever get to know. And then I start to form a plan of all the things I need to do to figure out this thing called life and what it means for me.

That night, however, I use the private plane that now belongs to me to go to Ryder's final playoff game in New York City. He won't expect me. I find my seat right behind home plate. *The power of money*. Got to love it. Wearing his jersey and his team hat, I wink when he walks out to the pitcher's mound. I owe him this. Damn, he looks good in uniform. I'm not sure if he sees me, but the way I cheer like the cheerleader I'd never been, I'm certain at some point he figures it out.

He pitches a near perfect game until the eighth inning. The crowd stands in ovation as he leaves the field. Our eyes finally meet, and I bite my lip. He's so beautiful it hurts my heart. There is so much to say, but now isn't the time. My feelings for him run so deep, I can't be selfish and burden him with my shit, especially if I'm still unclear with where life will lead me.

When the closer does his job and they win, the crowd rushes the field. I use that time of chaos to discreetly leave because I haven't earned my right to be here, but I had to come anyway. And I can't leave this time without saying something.

Me: Good game, Cowboy. Be safe as you celebrate. But most of all, have fun!

I turn off my phone for fear he'd text me back. Such the coward I am. He's my weakness. And I have a lot to do before I'm worthy of him. That's if he's still on the market when I am.

RYDER

The way my heart soars when I see her wearing my jersey and hat almost matches the high I get when I receive the standing ovation as I leave the field after the eighth inning. It's been my dream ever since I can remember to pitch in the playoffs, and then the World Series. Here I am living it. But the thing that beats it all is seeing Gina acting like my greatest fan in the world.

It was a huge surprise to find her sitting behind home plate. She didn't tell me she was coming to the game, so when I walked out to the mound and got ready to throw my first pitch, imagine my shock to see her sitting there. And there was no mistaking that dark hair, even though she wore the cap pulled down low over her eyes. Then when I threw my first strike, I almost chuckled because she flew to her feet as if I'd struck the batter out. When I did, I thought she was going to climb over the high fence behind the catcher's box. I never had any idea she was such a crazed fan. If the umpire called a ball, she was quick to boo him, too. Not only was she a fairy princess, she was a passion princess in every way possible.

The game could not have gone any better. We did everything right, and our opponent did everything wrong. In the end, we won five to zip. My pitching was near perfect with the exception of two base hits in two separate innings.

After the game, I scan the seat where Gina was sitting but don't see her. Maybe she went up to wait on me, so I head to the lockers to hunt my phone. As soon as I get there, I'm road blocked by the manager and other players congratulating me on my great pitching. Ms. Cougar herself stops and has that lecherous look in her eyes, the one I've come to despise, so I know this won't be a short conversation.

"Great work, Ryder. You're our ace after all. Still not interested in my proposal?"

Dipping my head, I say, "I'm flattered, ma'am, but I'm in a relationship."

"Hmm, that's curious."

"How so?"

"Your friend, Gina. That's her name, isn't it? And don't worry. I keep track of all my boys to make sure the Cougar name isn't sullied. This is our first year of the franchise."

"Yes, ma'am." I'm feeling a little uneasy. It's more than a bit creepy she keeps tabs on us like that.

"I watched her leave the stadium from my view in the box. I wondered why she wasn't in the team box with the other players' wives and significant others. Trouble in paradise?"

"Not that I'm aware of." There's no way I'm spilling my personal life to Cougar Whitestone.

"Well, no matter." She pats my arm. "I guess you don't value your position on the team then. Looks like I'll be negotiating a trade for you after this season ends, after all. And you are aware of what that means, aren't you?"

"I am aware."

She pats my arm again, this time with a smile that shows her little teeth. I swear, they have points on each of them. "Good. Then you don't mind being fifth in line for ace, do you?"

There's not any reason to answer. I don't mind being an infrequent starter as long as I don't have to deal with her harassment shit anymore. As soon as she walks away, I make a beeline for my duffle to dig out my phone. Talking to Gina is the only thing that will calm me down and give my addled brain some clarity. When I tap on my phone, a text lights it up, and it's from my girl. As I read it, my world collapses into a heap at my feet. She's gone and didn't even bother to stay to congratulate me in person. She only left a short text to basically tell me to be safe and have fun. What the fuck? Why bother to come at all? The high I've been experiencing vanishes and turns to anger mixed with confusion and hurt. She's playing games, and the only game I play is baseball. I'm a straight shooter, so I don't have a fucking clue as to how to deal with this shit.

"Ryder, you okay?" Robinson stands next to me, waving his hand in front of my face.

"Um, yeah. Fine. Why?"

"I've been asking you the same question three times now."

"Oh, sorry. What did you want?"

"Are you ever going to shower? The guys are all going to the party tonight, and everyone's getting ready to leave."

"Yeah, I'm going now."

"Okay," he says. "I'll wait on you. My ex took my car, so I'll need a ride."

"Jesus, Robinson, when is your divorce going to be over?"

"Probably never. She wants everything I own, so my lawyer is giving her a lot. I need to buy a car. I gave her mine yesterday."

"How did you get here?"

"Uber."

I shake my head. The man has shit for brains. "How long did you know you were giving your car up?"

"A week."

"Why didn't you go and buy another?"

He shrugs his meaty shoulders. Dumbass. He deserves not having a car. Maybe he'll be gone when I come out, but no such luck. The locker room is nearly empty, except for Robinson, a few other players, and some of the janitorial people.

After I dress, we head to my car. The entire time, I notice he's been on his phone texting. "Who're you chatting with?"

"A chick. I saw her in the stands, and one of the ball boys snagged her number for me. I'm having her come to the party."

"You're a shit, you know?"

His head snaps in my direction. "Why?"

"This is why you're getting divorced. Because you pick up random women. Why don't you meet them in a normal way? Like get properly introduced and not have the damn ball boy get their number at a game. What? Are you sending sexts to her?"

He looks away for a second and then says, "Yeah, isn't that what you do?"

"No, I don't do that. Idiot. Please tell me you don't send any of them naked pics of yourself or your dick."

His mouth gapes open.

"Jesus Christ, Robinson, your junk is gonna end up online with a caption next to it that says—Max Robinson's cock. You'd better hope it's a big dick, my man, and not some four inch wiener that some chick wants to make fun of."

His eyes drop down to his zipper, and he says, "Fuck. What should I do?" He has a panicked look about him.

"One, stop doing stupid shit like this. Two, stop fucking around with anything that has a pussy. Three, stop sending pictures of your naked ass self to every fucking piece of ass you meet."

"Fuck."

"Dammit, Robinson, if your wife gets wind of this shit before your divorce is final, you'll end up with zip. How can you be so damn idiotic? And for once in your life, think about your kids."

"My kids?" This guy doesn't have a clue.

"Yes! How would you like it if your kids found out about this?"

"But they're so young," he insists.

"They won't be four and six forever." By now I want to shake him. "Maybe you need to move in with your parents."

He looks at me like I'm the dumbass now, but whatever. We drive to the party, and sure enough, there's his groupie hanging out by the door.

"That her?"

"Yeah." He grins.

"You're on your own, and good luck when you don't have a dime to your name and your kids won't have a thing to do with you."

"Huh?"

"Never mind." I think of Gina and how she didn't know her mom and wasn't close to her dad. I really feel sorry for Robinson's kids. He walks up to the young woman, who's waiting for him, and gives her a goofy grin. I think he has the maturity level of a sixteen-year-old.

He stands outside with the young girl, so I pass them and head through the doors, hoping that Ms. Cougar leaves me alone. My destination is the bar where I can grab a few shots, but I'm surprised to see my family here. I knew they were trying to get here, but Riley said she didn't think Mom and Dad could make it in.

Mom rushes up to me, and I feel like that kid again in Little League who just hit his first home run.

"Ryder, let me look at you." She pulls back, and it's like looking in a mirror when I see her eyes. She smiles, and it's full of pride. "You did it, and I couldn't be any prouder than I am right now."

"Thanks, Mom."

Dad is standing next to her, and when she lets me go, he gives me a man hug and pounds me on the back. "I've never seen anything better, son. You made this old man proud."

"Old man, my ass. You're not even fifty-five yet."

Riley barrels into me with a tackle hug, and I almost fall on my ass. "Jesus, are you training for the Rockets? Fletcher said they were looking for a defensive end, but I didn't know you took him seriously."

"Shut it, bro. I'm just so excited for your sloppy ass, I can't stand it."

"I love you, too, old lady."

She leans in so only I can hear and asks, "Are you good?" Her eyes dig into mine.

"Um, not really. What do you know about Gina? I take it that's what you mean?"

"Yeah, pretty much."

"Ryder! Get your ass over here. Now!" I look up to see David motioning to me. I stick a finger in the air, giving him the universal *wait a minute* sign.

"No, get over here now!"

Turning back to my family, I say, "I'm sorry. He's a little insistent."

"Go. We'll be fine right here," Mom says.

"Come with me. Then I won't have to stay so long."

Mom puts her hand on my shoulder. "Ryder, you just pitched the best game of your life, and you're getting ready to play in the World Series. This is something you've worked for your entire life. We can wait a few minutes. We'll be here a few days. Now, go and celebrate this victory."

"Thanks, Mom."

Even with all the handshakes and back pats, the one thing that I miss the most is my girl. And, yes, she is mine. She should be here, right by my side, helping me celebrate. Without her, I have to wonder if I would have pitched the same game that I did. Knowing she was there helped me throw with perfection. Maybe it was because I wanted to make her proud, or maybe it was because I wanted to show off my mad skills. Whatever, it worked. But now I'm hollow and empty inside, and I miss her like a crazy fucker. The party in me is gone, and all I want to do is go home and drown my sorrows, alone. I hate to admit this, but I don't even care that my parents are here, and that's a shitty thing to say or even think.

Putting a stick of rebar in my spine, I down a couple of shots and use Mom, Dad, and Riley as an excuse to leave the screaming group of testosterone that surrounds us.

My family grins at me as I wobble back toward them.

"Looks like someone's had a few," Riley says. She sticks a finger in my ribs and pokes me hard.

"Ow. Stop that." She's always known exactly where my tender spots are.

Mom looks at Dad and says, "Some things never change."

"Hey, do you all mind leaving? I could use a bite to eat."

"Not at all. You sure you want to leave?"

Right then, Ms. Cougar sidles up to us. "Ryder, are you going to introduce us?" She puts her arm around me and acts entirely too chummy for my taste. I try to shrug out of her grasp, but every time I move, she goes with me.

"Ms. Whitestone, this is my family." I make all the introductions, and she gushes over me like I was the greatest thing in the world. She hangs on my every last word, and my mom stares at me, as does Riley. They both think something is up.

When there's a small break in the conversation, I finally say, "It was nice talking with you, but we were just heading out. My parents are only here for a few days, so I want to spend some private time with them."

"I understand. By the way, did you tell them about

the trade?"

"No, I haven't had the chance." What a fucking bitch. I need to get out of this team. She's a flaming whore.

"I see. Well, enjoy your evening."

We leave, and on the way out, my mom asks, "Trade?"

"I'll explain. Let's get out of here."

Right by the door, we pass Robinson with his tongue jammed down that girl's throat. I grab his arm and pull him off her. "Would you straighten up? You're going to lose everything you have if you don't pull your shit together."

He looks at me with glazed eyes, and I have to wonder if he's on drugs. "Are you on anything?" I ask.

"Huh?"

"Did you take anything? Drugs?"

His damn eyes can't even focus. I look at the girl and ask, "Did you give him anything?"

"No." And to be honest, she doesn't look like she has an active brain cell in her head.

"Robinson, look at me." He stares for a second, and I ask him again, "Did you take drugs?"

"No, just that." He points to the table next to where they stand.

"Jesus, how much did you drink?" He motions to the bottle of tequila, and three quarters of it are gone.

I ask my parents if they can find the restaurant because I need Riley to drive us. Even I've had a bit too much to drive, and Robinson needs to go home. I order the girl an Uber, and we take Robinson to where he's been staying. Once I get him inside, we head to the restaurant.

"He's a dumbass." I explain his circumstances. "I'm not sure he'll ever learn."

"But at least you tried," Mom says. "So, what's this about a trade?"

I groan and tell them about the vicious cougar attacks I've been experiencing.

My mom nearly jumps out of her seat. "That's sexual harassment."

"Yeah, and who would believe me? She'd just deny it, or even turn the tables and say I was the one harassing her. I have no proof. And honestly, right now, I would welcome a trade to be away from her. She's a nutcase."

Dad stares, and he's pissed. His face always takes on an angular look, as his cheeks appear more chiseled somehow. His mouth turns down, and then he speaks, "Ryder, you can't let her push you out like this. You earned your place as ace, and if you're traded you'll be in the fourth or fifth spot, depending on where you end up."

"Guess I'll have to take my chances, because playing under that woman is not worth it to me anymore."

"Please, son, let's see if we can take legal action," Dad begs.

"Then my reputation will really be toast."

Riley steps up to my aid. "He's right, Dad. I see where

your thoughts are, but Ryder would be completely screwed, and no one would touch him after that."

The waiter stops by to take our order, and out of habit I get the bone in ribeye, medium rare. I'm not even sure if I'll be able to eat. I hear the low hum of chatter around me, but I can't help but wonder where Gina is tonight. Is she happy, or sad? What's she doing? Who's she with?

Riley kicks me under the table. When I look up, she gives a slight shake to her head.

Mom says, "So I hear Cassie and Fletcher are going to have a little one."

"That's the news," Riley says.

"How exciting for them," I say.

"Oh, and I almost forgot. How many tickets to the World Series can you get?" Mom asks.

"I don't know. Why?"

Mom reaches for a warm piece of bread that the waiter just delivered and says, "Your cousin, Kaycee, wants to come."

"Kaycee? Isn't she like twelve?"

Riley leans across the table and punches me. "No, she's not twelve, you dork. She's twenty-one."

"Already?"

"Yes," Mom says. "And she's probably going to be skiing in the next Olympics."

"No shit."

"Watch your mouth, Ryder," Mom admonishes.

"Yes, ma'am. Sorry."

"Anyway, Kaycee just retuned a week or two ago from Chile. You know that's where they train in the summer. She has a month off before the big snows hit out West, so she wants to come and watch. That is, if you have any extra tickets."

"Sure. I'll see what I can do. I know Fletcher will want to come when he can, Cassie, you all, and—" I would've said Gina, but I doubt there's any chance of that.

After dinner, we all head back to my place. As soon as Mom and Dad go to bed, I beg Riley to tell me what she knows.

"I talked to her, and she told me she needed to get some things straight with her life. Ryder, be patient. It's all so new to her. She didn't say as much, but I gather with everything that happened, she's trying to sort it all out. We didn't talk more than a few minutes, but I think she was trying to let me know how much she cares."

"Uh huh. So much that she couldn't stick around to tell me herself." Riley looks at me with pity, and that's the last thing I need. "Stop it, Riley. I don't want that from anyone, least of all you."

"I know how much you care for her."

"No, you can't possibly know that."

"Okay, maybe not, but I do know you love her. And that's saying a lot. I'm pretty damn sure she loves you, too."

I snort. "Well, she has a fucked-up way of showing it."

"Ryder, she wasn't raised like we were."

"True, but when you show someone how much you care, the last thing you do is turn your back on them."

"You're not getting it. At all," Riley insists.

"Guess not. But I'll tell you what I am getting. She stuck her fist inside my chest and ripped out my heart. I got that part just fine. I'm done. I can't deal with that again."

"Oh, Ryder, I'm sorry. But I wish you would trust me on this."

"Sorry, the only person I'm trusting where Gina's involved is myself." I turn away and head to bed, even though I seriously doubt I'll be able to sleep tonight.

GINA

Hours Before

There has been so much to do. So many decisions to make that will affect the rest of my life. The first one was to get a new lawyer. No offense to my mother's, but he's been a little too possessive for my liking. And maybe in a different time I would have given him the time of day, but there's another man who makes my heart pound in my chest. So a headstrong female is assigned to me, and I'm all about girl power.

That is one of the many things I had to take care of, including deciding the fate of my mother's estate. It's something she purchased recently, wanting to ride out her days in Florida, where the climate is good all year round. So I put it up for sale after spending time with an estate seller and my lawyer going through the things I would let go. It turns out ninety-five percent of it is going up for auction at month's end.

There are several portraits and paintings I decide to keep. I let go of most of the furniture as none of it really appeals to me.

It's surreal to be back in my tiny living room after the vastness of her estate. I wonder how I could ever leave this place. This is my first apartment. It's home, even though the clutter has been organized. And what about that? Ryder paid money for me to get to this point, and now I plan to box everything up.

This is one decision I haven't been able to make. A knock comes at the door and takes me out of my misery. My steps falter when I think it might be Ryder. I peer through the hole and open the door.

"Riley."

She glances down at me from her slightly taller height.

"I warned you what I'd do if you broke my brother's heart."

I turn around as she pushes her way inside. Flattening myself to the door, I cross my arms over my chest. "Here to fight me?"

She spins around and mimics my stance.

"Let me warn you. I have a mean right hook," I tease.

Rolling her eyes, she says, "And let me warn you. I've been doing kickboxing for the last two years."

"Sounds like we are at a standoff."

"Maybe," Riley begins. "I, at least, want to know why you dumped my brother."

Of course, she does.

"I didn't dump him. I cut him loose, temporarily. And that's only because I thought it was fair. How could I ask him to wait for me when I wasn't sure how long it would take me to figure things out? I'm not good at the relationship thing. I don't know how to be considerate. I'm used to coming and going as I please."

The vomiting of words freed me from some of the guilt I'd been feeling. She deflates and sits on my sofa. I do the same.

"I get it. I'm independent, too. I'm not sure I'll ever let a man get that close to me." She sighs. "Still, if you're truly done with my brother, be a woman and tell him."

Grinding my teeth, I bite back a retort. "I deserve that. I care for him. Hell, it's more than that. He's made me feel. He's treated me better than anyone. Well, except my first and that time it didn't feel right."

"Who's that?"

If she had been anyone else, I might not have answered.

"Mark," I remind her.

I wait for the flash of recognition in her eyes.

"Fletcher's best friend?" Nodding, I wait. "Figures."

"Figures why?" I ask.

"You and I are a lot alike. I used to crush on him when I was younger."

"And?" Because I know there's more.

"He told you?"

"Not really," I admit.

She lets out a breath. "He's hot, but you know that. Whenever we came into town to visit my aunt and uncle, he'd be around. I remember him having a girlfriend one summer. And the next, he was brokenhearted. That must have been you."

It still bothers me that I hurt him. I loved him, just not in that way.

"We were better off as friends. He sees that."

"Leaving a trail of broken hearts. Even I'm not that bad."

"Being a realist. It's kind of hard to screw a guy when he feels more like your brother than your boyfriend."

She nods and continues with her story.

"True. Anyway, one night, we were sitting on the tree swing. Well, I was. We'd been drinking, and not old enough to. Beer," she explains. "And he kissed me or I kissed him. But that was it."

"It was?"

She gives me a noncommittal shrug.

"He's a good guy," I say. "You should go for it."

"And take your sloppy seconds. No thanks."

I laugh. "It was once too many years ago. It doesn't even count."

"I don't know. I have bigger issues. A charity event has come up, and I need to find a caddy since I won't have one in another month."

"Oh, that's right. I remember Ryder mentioning something about your caddy quitting. When is the event?"

She lifts her eyes to the ceiling. "Thank God the sponsors set it for after the World Series. They are trying to bring money in, and I don't want to pull out because it's for the Make-A-Wish Foundation. They're done with their normal campaign, but a child who has just been diagnosed with terminal brain cancer wants to play a round of golf with the pros. Because she's not expected to live out the year, they are putting this together rather quickly. I'm lucky to have been invited."

"See, it's that kind of shit that puts life in perspective. You should do it."

"I can't." Her laugh is humorless. "I can't very well lug my clubs around by myself."

"Can't you just hire someone else?"

"It's not that easy. Caddies are hard to come by."

An idea hits me. "You should hire Mark. He has nothing better to do." When she frowns, I add, "His company went under. He's been following me around like a mother hen. You're the distraction he needs."

"Caddies are trained."

"He's an excellent golfer," I insist.

"There's more to being a caddy than knowing how to play the game."

This idea keeps sounding better and better in my head. I'm quick with a response. "But you said yourself, the season is over. This is for charity. What harm could it do?"

She exhales. "I'll think about it, but you have to do something for me."

"What's that?"

"The last game of the pennant is tonight, and Ryder is starting."

"I know. I've gone to each of his games."

She stares at me. "I know. Which is why I can't understand why you are giving him the silent treatment." When I open my mouth to explain, she cuts in, "It doesn't matter to me. You should explain to him. Anyway, when they win, there will be a party. You should come."

"I'll think about it."

Getting to her feet, she says, "I hope you will. I'll text you the details. And remember one thing, a guy like my brother won't be alone forever."

I nod and walk her to the door. That's the risk I've taken over these last several weeks.

"About that sex club. You never took me, and my season's over." She winks.

"You still want me to?"

"Hell yeah."

After she's gone, I head downstairs to talk to Sam. Although, I'm not exactly sure where I'll end up, there are a few things I do know. The bar is hopping because of the game tonight. He asks me to come back later. I knew things would be busy. I hadn't expected the rush to come on so early. Then again, this is the first time we have a hometown team from the Carolinas in the World Series.

Instead, I think about traffic and the two and a half hour drive to the stadium and opt to use my plane to fly me into town and a car service to the stadium. I get ready and put Ryder's jersey on and pull my hair back.

My seat behind the plate costs more than my annual

salary at the bar. The fact that I had the money to spend disconcerts me. I'm still not used to the wealth that has befallen me.

The pre-game show includes having the players out signing autographs for kids and fans alike. I pull my hat down and try not to be seen when he nears the area in which I'm sitting. But I have nothing to worry about. The kids and women getting him to sign their jerseys is enough for him not to notice me.

I try not to let jealousy get the best of me. He'd been mine, but I'd given him up.

"It's a shame you're single," I hear a woman practically yell to him. "You really shouldn't be."

"I shouldn't," he says, to the delight of all the women who hear him.

Turning away, I'm grateful I tucked my hair under my hat. I hope the jeans and combat boots I wear will throw him off, and he won't figure out it's me. Besides, he is over twenty feet away.

By the time the game begins, long after the players go back inside to the locker rooms, I'm full of beer and a hotdog. I've been hit on and had drinks rain down on my arm as people who are already sloshed jostle in the chaos that is the first playoff game.

After the crowd dies down when the players take the field, everything is silent. Ryder enters, and everyone gets to their feet. The whole time, I don't yell or cheer. That's the plan for the entire game. I don't want him to lose his concentration. My stomach is in knots because I know what this game could mean for him.

If they win the pennant, he'll earn a place in baseball history. Remaining stoically nail-biting quiet turns out to be a good choice. He pitches another for the record books. A no-hitter that carries him to the ninth inning before the manager pulls him in favor of their closer.

The ovation he gets is one I can see being a theme every time he plays in the future. There is greatness in him beyond anything I ever let myself see, and I'm so fucking proud. I slip away as my heart breaks. I don't know what to do still, so I fly home and head back to the bar and talk to Sam. He's been sort of a father figure to me these past few years.

I explain everything, including my ideas for the future. I'd bounced them off of Cassie first, and she also agreed. Sam's agreement only solidifies my thoughts.

"Go get him, kid," he says as he envelops me in a hug.

Out of everything he said, I'm now excited about the future. But everything hinges on one man. He's the last piece of the puzzle I need to put in place.

Upstairs, I put on a dress. I don't know why, as I hardly ever wear one like this. It's summery and not made of leather or lace. It's respectable if not for the fact that it's shorter than something you'd where to church on Sunday. I frivolously use the plane I never asked for to get back to Charlotte and another car service to get me to my destination. It's convenient. And ultimately, he's worth every penny I spend.

The room is filled to the brim when I arrive. I can hardly make out the floor color from the density of the crowd. I move with the tide until I spot him holding court in a far corner. A pretty petite woman is near, and when she wraps her arms around his neck and he bends down, I'm sick. I can't turn back and flee. I'm pushed forward until I reach a back door and spill out into the night.

So far, the backyard is empty. I spot a gazebo out in the distance. I push my legs to move when I find it hard to walk. Stumbling forward, I make my way there as tears gather in my eyes. What a fool I'd been. How could I have been so stupid?

"Gina."

I turn, just as I reach the steps. For balance, I hold on to the wood railing, seeing Ryder jogging toward me. Furiously, I wipe at my eyes, not caring if my makeup smudges.

"Hey, congratulations," I say with false cheer when he catches up.

Holding out my hand, he gives me a puzzled look as if my arm is a foreign object.

"Is that what we are now?"

"What do you mean? I'm being gracious. I wouldn't want your date to get the wrong idea about us."

"Date?" His face screws up. "Kaycee, my cousin."

"Petite, pretty, and a second ago you were about to kiss her..."

"On the cheek and she's not my date." He takes another step, crowding me in the darkness.

His hand lands on my outer thigh and slides up under my dress. I suck in a hiss. Once he registers what I'm not wearing, he stares in my eyes.

"Surprise," I say weakly.

"You've been walking around like this... bare."

I clamp my teeth together and force a smile that must look like I have the shits. I lift my shoulders and let them fall.

He doesn't waste time. His lips find mine, and it's sweeter than honey and hotter than fire. Hoisting me up, he climbs the stairs and finds the darkest corner. I can hear him work at opening his pants.

"Your shoulder," I protest when he finally gives me a second to breathe.

"It's okay. I have another one."

It's true. He lifts me with his left arm, and it's seconds when his fingers dip inside me.

"Wet," he mutters.

"Always," I admit.

Then the crown of his cock nudges at my opening. My back slides down the wood, and I fear a splinter has caught me. It's forgotten as he presses inside. Audibly, I gasp. I've missed his invasions. Whenever he fucks me, I feel conquered.

"I'm mad at you, Gina. I can't be nice tonight."

"Give me your worst," I beg.

He plunges into me so hard, I see stars. That might be partly because I dropped my head back from the thrill of how good he felt. The wood behind me wasn't pliable, and the knock to the skull I received will probably leave a bruise.

He buries his face in the crook of my neck.

"Damn, Gina. I've missed this. I've missed you. I will never let you go this time."

"I'm not going anywhere, ever."

I'm surprised by my words. I hadn't been sure until now. But now I am. I love this man, or something so close to it. I can't determine the difference.

He rocks into me, and each thrust brings me closer to an emotional edge I hadn't known existed. But this time I'm ready. Never before in my life have I been this ready.

As the orgasm tears through me, I confess, "I love you."

RYDER

"And it's about fucking time." Her words work their way through me and settle into my heart, wedging their way into my soul, sealing our fate forever. She's mine and will be for life. "I love you, too, you beautiful crazy woman." My lips seal the deal as they press against hers, and she swallows another moan. I set her down on the steps.

"You know how to spoil a girl," she purrs.

"Trust me. You haven't seen anything yet. Promise me something."

"Anything."

"You won't ever run from me again." She leans back, and even though her eyes are still soft from the orgasm I just gave her, I can see there's something she needs to say. "What is it, princess?"

Her fingers lightly skim over my cheek, and she says, "I didn't leave because I wanted to. I did it because I had to. There were things I needed to do, to take care of."

And she explains. But the kicker is, she was at every one of my games. She watched me pitch every ball.

"Why didn't you let me know?"

"I didn't want you to know. I would've caved, Ryder. You have to know that."

Her bottom lip trembles just slightly, but enough that I notice, so I lean in to kiss the quivering away. "No more sadness or regrets. From this point on, it's you and me. Together. Forever. You're going to be Gina Wilde. I hope you don't have a problem with that."

"Wait. Don't you think you should ask me first?"

"I don't know. I'm not sure I want you to have a choice." She finally notices the curve of my lips, and I'm rewarded with a solid poke in the ribs. "Hey, a man has to have a plan. That's all I'm saying here."

She peeks out at me from under a fringe of dark lashes, and that sexy look gets me rock hard again.

"Shit, Gina." I put her hand on my cock, and she grins.

"Won't people notice we're gone?"

"I'm sure they will. But a quickie?" I beg her for more. "I've been deprived of your sweet pussy for these last several weeks, and look what's happened."

Her throaty laugh doesn't help either. But her hand does. Long, tight strokes leave me hungry for what's between her legs, so I use my fingers to spread her lips and mark her in return. She's still soaked from our lovemaking a few minutes ago, and it makes me moan. "God, you are so ready again. You feel like warm, wet silk." I brush her hand off me and spread her thighs apart, wrapping them around me as I slide my cock deep inside her warmth.

"I'll never get enough of you. Of this. Of us. I want us to go home and be together for the entire night. I've missed our nights together, with you next to me."

She murmurs things to me, but I'm lost in her tight heat, her silky cunt, and all I want to do is fuck her.

"Harder, Ryder. I need it hard."

"Like this?" I thrust hard, lifting her off the step each time.

"Yes."

It doesn't take long for either of us to find our release. Afterward, she lets out a long bellowing laugh.

"We're like two teenagers. Look at us. My dress looks like shit."

"Sexy shit." Sitting back on my heels, I let my eyes roam her. "I love it when you're messy after we've just made love."

"So, we've gone from fucking to making love, have we?"

The question concerns me. Not for my feelings, because I know exactly where my heart is, but because I don't want her running off scared again. "Can I be honest here?"

"Ryder, if you ever give me anything but honesty, I can promise you, you won't like the outcome."

"Fair enough. So then, being with you is an adventure. Every single time. And, yes, we fuck. Like crazy. And I wouldn't have it any other way. But somehow, I believe my heart got wrapped up in you from the very first time, so even though we do fuck, and we do it right, we also make love right, too. I hope I'm making sense here." I'm pretty damn sure I just hit a home run, because even though the light is so dim, her smile lights up the entire stairway we're sitting on.

With her smile still in place, I say, "Come on." I realize she'll need the restroom to make herself look presentable, so I pull her up, kiss her one more time, and add, "I would stay here all night with you, but we can't. So, let's go back to the party."

"One thing," she says softly.

"What's that?" I stare into her deep brown eyes.

"We didn't use protection."

I shrug, even though I hadn't thought about it. Caught up in greed and need, I just went for her. "Maybe I just got you pregnant. Not like it matters. You're mine, and the baby will be mine. And I'm clean."

She narrows her eyes. "And that's that?"

"Yeah."

"You didn't ask my status."

"I figured you'd tell me."

Nodding, she says, "I'm clean. I've never..." She waves an absent hand. "Never without with anyone, ever. But I get tested anyway."

"So we're good."

Shaking her head, I lead her to the restroom first. From her squeals, my swimmers were falling victim to gravity. She wants to get to the bathroom before it happens, panty-less and all.

I wait for her in the hall, surprisingly calm at the thought of her with my child, though she tells me she's on the pill. When she emerges, she looks like a breath of fresh air wrapped around a warm summer day in the middle of winter.

"God, I love you. You are the greatest thing that ever happened to me, including baseball."

She slants her head and stares. "Wow, that's really some comment."

I put my palms on each side of her face. "I am sincere in whatever I say to you."

She rewards me by throwing her arms around my neck and kissing me.

"If I'd known that's all it took to get a response from you like that, I'd have said it sooner."

We head back and join the party, where the rest of my family is. I introduce Gina to Kaycee and chuckle about her thinking my cousin was my date.

"Gina, Kaycee just got back from Chile. She's on the U.S. Ski Team and was in training for the upcoming season."

"Oh, that's cool. I never thought about where skiers trained in the summer."

"Yeah," Kaycee says, "we go to the other side of the equator. But in mid-November, we'll start getting snow, hopefully, on our mountains here. So this is my time off."

"Nice. What's your event?"

"Downhill, giant slalom and super-G." Kaycee is chirpy like a bird when she talks about her sport. I hadn't seen her in a while, and all I can think about is that ten-year-old kid who was always a daredevil.

"This one," I point to my cousin, "was never afraid of anything. If there was a tree, she'd climb it. If there was a hill, she'd ride her bike down it like her hair was on fire."

"Yep, that's me," she says. "I like to go fast."

Gina says, "You must to ski that kind of stuff. How fast do you go?"

"Very. The men go faster, though, because they weigh more. Honestly, I don't really want to know. I think it jinxes me."

"So, Olympics?" Gina asks.

"I'm hoping."

"Gina, don't let her fool you. She's one of the top skiers in the U.S. If she doesn't make it, it'll be because of something we won't mention." When Gina looks at me curiously, I shake my head. It's totally bad luck to talk about injuries in front of an athlete, especially one like Kaycee. The danger of being a downhill skier is incredible.

Riley runs behind Gina and pinches her butt. Gina spins around, but Riley has already moved next to me. When Gina turns back around, Riley stands there with an innocent look on her face, but she can't hold it before she cracks up. Then the two women are hugging. They whisper some things to each other, but I have no idea what they are. And I won't ask either. I'm only happy to see them with their arms linked together, chatting away as if they were best friends. I'm not sure what I would've done had they not gotten along.

Soon, we're joined by the rest of the Wilde clan. My parents, my aunt and uncle, Fletcher and Cassie, Mark, and even Fletcher's little brother, Chase, came in from Europe to see the game. I'm so proud when I introduce my girl to everyone for the first time.

The party is in full swing. The team is having a great time with each of their family members, and all of the coaches are present, the manager and so on, and I look up to see Cougar Whitestone walking in the door. I'm pretty sure my night is about to take a turn for the worse.

Spoons clink against crystal, and she steps up to the front of the room. A round of applause goes through the room, with the men chanting, "Whitestone, Whitestone, Whitestone." I can't bring myself to join in. She makes a few comments about what a great team we are and how she always knew we could win the pennant. She saw that magic in us early on and knew with hard work and effort we would do it. Blah, blah, blah. The cheers and shouts fill the room. The men are on a victory high. Not me. I know what drives this bitch, and it's not this. It's preying on people her money can control.

Gina's small hand is in mine, and she gives mine a little squeeze every now and then. She doesn't know what the cougar woman is all about because I haven't told her. And I don't plan on it unless I have to. But then when she opens up her next line, I know my road to victory was only a few minutes on the mountaintop. Whitestone doesn't give a rat's ass about the welfare of this team. She only wants what makes her happy.

"So," she continues to speak, "I have the pleasure of announcing that we will be making a trade with the New York Yankees. Ryder Wilde will be moving from the Cougars and heading up to New York." If ever there was a room where crickets chirped, it was here. The expression on Gina's face tells me more than I care to know. Her home is North Carolina.

GINA

New York, the name of the city keeps running through my brain as a ruckus erupts from the crowd. They, like me, aren't thrilled with the news. I block out the words and shouts coming from the crowd. The smile plastered to my face is for Ryder. I don't want him to know what I'm feeling. What am I feeling?

"Gina." I glance up to my other side to find Cassie's worried expression. "Are you okay?"

I blink a few times, and her face comes into focus. "Yeah, chica. What's up?"

Her eyes narrow. The plastic smile I've managed to maintain blooms into something more real. My best friend, my rock, my family. She's here. And everything else is good. New York isn't that far, and I have access to a freakin' plane now. Fletcher and Cassie have managed to do it. The world is a much smaller place now.

"You looked like something was bothering you," she

says, as Ryder is whisked away.

"I'm fine, really." I take several steps back, distancing myself from the chaos, leaving her with it.

Swallowed up by his family, I watch as Ryder is bombarded with words and questions as I continue to melt into the background. Soon he's totally out of sight, and I find a seat.

"Hey, are you okay?"

Riley stands over me. I nearly jump out of my dress because I thought she was with the others.

"You're the second person to ask me that tonight. And I'm fine."

"He didn't know," she says.

Tilting my head back, I realize that was the question that had been circling in my head. Then he's there.

"Gina."

I find the will to curve my lips. "Congratulations," I muster.

"Are you ready to get out of here?"

As I nod frantically, he helps me to my feet. Riley still wears a worried expression. I really must look like shit.

Unfortunately, we pass the owner along the way.

There isn't a thought when I tug my hand free from Ryder's and march up to the woman who thinks she's destroying his life.

I get so close my finger is a millisecond away from drilling into her nose.

"You are so stupid. You traded away one of the best players this team has."

"She's right about that," a big guy, who I think is Robinson, says.

I ignore him and continue with my rant. "All because he wouldn't fuck you, you stretch-faced old hag."

"If that's what he told you—"

She's not getting the floor. It's my turn. "He didn't have to tell me anything. I saw those staged pictures of your lips on his. And when he didn't give you what you wanted, you made good on your threat to trade him. And he's too good of a person to call you out on your sexual harassment."

"I'll fuck you if Ryder can stay," Robinson calls out from somewhere behind me.

"But he doesn't need you. You'll eat your trade when he wins the pennant for the Yankees. I'm only sad for all the great guys here that are stuck with you."

I didn't know I'd balled my fist until Ryder had me around the waist telling me not to hit his former boss.

Before I know it, the conversation melts away. Fresh air greets me before I'm in Ryder's car.

In anticipation of leaving with Ryder, I hadn't asked the driver of the car service to hang around.

"You didn't have to do that," he says, squeezing my hand.

"I'm sorry. She fucking smirked at me, and I just had to say something."

"Thank you for saying what I couldn't. It means more to me than I can say."

"She deserved worse." I try to smile, but it doesn't

last.

Ryder seems to understand my need for quiet. He doesn't add anything else and lets me brood in my thoughts. I'm back to thinking about New York. It's like the ground beneath my feet is shaky with the aftershocks of an earthquake. How much more change can I take before I break?

Eventually, we pull into a gated underground garage. I feel air lifted because I don't remember leaving the car and making it to his floor, my mind is spinning. I thought the plan was made, and now everything is changing again. He opens the door, and the condo is large but not ostentatious.

"What a place," I mutter.

"It's more than what I need with two floors and over four thousand square feet. But it was the only place available in this building where I wanted to be at the time, which is why Riley lives with me."

He escorts me around. My eyes travel to the open concept living room, dining room, and kitchen area. He could throw a party with maybe a hundred guests no problem, but what do I know. "Nice. Who decorated?"

"Don't like it?" he asks.

The floors are dark wood, the furnishing tasteful and not the museum kind. It certainly differs from the palace my birth mother lived in. That place had a sterile quality that made me feel out of place. Ryder's home is different. It has a homey feeling like you can put your feet up without fear of being yelled at. Creams and blues are the primary colors, and my eyes soak it all in.

"It's pretty, but you didn't answer my question. Who had an eye for decorating, you? Or was it Riley?"

"Neither of us. My agent hired a decorator who got the place ready for me."

"Must be nice."

He stops me halfway to the stairs. "Don't," he warns. "I see it in your eyes."

Meeting his gray ones, I say, "See what?"

He studies me for a moment longer. "You look like you're going to run."

This time, he's wrong. I'm not running away, but toward him. Looping my arms around his neck, I press my mouth to his. Slipping my tongue between his parted lips, I pour all my feelings into him.

Strong hands that can throw a ball faster than any starting pitcher lock on my hips with a bruising grip.

"I told you I'd never run again. Make love to me, Ryder."

My back hits the stairwell wall, where he was taking me to see the second floor, and my dress disappears from my body in record time. His sister lives here, too, but I don't care. I can't wait a second longer to be closer to him.

"I'm not wasting time to find a bed to have you," he says, voice gruff.

A zipper pierces the silence of the house before my leg is hiked up and I rise. The head of his cock takes position at my entrance a second before I gasp as he pushes inside me. His hips work, he slides in and out of me because I'm always wet and ready for him. The angle of his thrusts change, and I have the vague sensation of falling. My butt hits a solid surface. The stairs are beneath me as he spreads my legs, pulling out. I want to protest, but then his mouth is on me. Moans and cries of pleasure leave my lips and would be so embarrassing if anyone heard.

"I'm going to come," I cry out.

His tongue and fingers work every part of my lower anatomy, igniting a fierce storm that vibrates through me. I'm pretty sure I scream. The fact that my back rams against the edge of a stair doesn't affect me at all. Then he's sliding home, and his mouth devours my shouts. I taste my orgasm on his tongue as another builds with his dick buried deep inside me. Another lightning strike rips through me and causes me to go limp. When he pulls free, I want to argue that he hadn't gotten his yet. Words must have left my lips.

"We're going to finish in my room."

My eyes flutter as we pass by doors. Nothing really registers. Loose and limber, I'm so sated, I want to close my eyes and drift off into oblivion as he carries me in his arms.

The cloud I land on feels heavenly. I start to roll from my back to lie on my stomach, but I'm caught in a web of hands that touch me places and stir another fire within me.

"You remember agreeing to marry me?"

"What?" I say as if I'm in a dream state.

"You heard me. We're going to get married, and you're going to stop taking the pill."

Fingers hook my chin, and he turns my open mouth to greet it with a kiss. Unable to think and breathe, he pulls back.

"Ryder," I start to protest.

"You don't have to say anything but yes."

So many arguments come to mind. But staring into his earnest eyes, I crush all of it down.

"Yes."

Out of all the decisions I've had to make, this one is the easiest. The one that feels right. And he's right, I already said yes. Had I really scared him into believing I was going to run?

"And now, you are going to let me have you here."

His fingers slide down to the crease of my ass. They circle an area I haven't let anyone have other than a small toy or a finger. It may seem crazy, but I hadn't saved myself for marriage. Oddly, in the back of my mind, I might have subconsciously saved that one part of me for the man I married.

"Yes, take me, Ryder."

He's prepared with lube. As his slick finger breaches that part of me, the sensation is strange, not in a bad way. With everything new, I feel when a second finger joins the first, and he scissors them inside me.

"Just breathe, baby."

I do as he asks, and he slides them in deeper. There

is a slight burning sensation, but Ryder isn't new at this. His other hand distracts me by circling my clit, driving me mad and wild.

"We're going to take this slow," he whispers. "Do you trust me?"

There is no need to think. "Yes."

"You know I love you, right?"

The question sounds dumb, then I get it. He's in need for reassurance because of my mini freak out. "Yes," I say again. "I love you, too."

His cock crosses my virgin barrier, and I suck in a lungful of air.

"No matter what happens, where this life leads us, I want you by my side." His gentle rocking and the pressure in a place that hasn't known such fullness seem like a backdrop to his words. "I'm going to make you happy. No matter what it takes."

His dexterous fingers glide into my pussy, adding to the fullness between my legs.

"I'll move to New York," I say. And I mean it. Although, I believe Riley when she said he didn't know. It really doesn't matter if he did or not. I love this man, hard. His balls slap my ass as he seats himself inside me. "Now shut up and fuck me."

He does just that. I'm taken to new heights, something I've never experienced with anyone else. I hadn't thought I could derive pleasure from this. But Ryder warms me up and soon I'm catching a wave that will crest like no other. His sure and even strokes at some point lose their rhythm. His thumb presses down on my clit, and I shatter beneath him. He follows me over that cliff, leaving us both breathless and satisfied.

My limbs are so wobbly; there is no way I can move. I'm so grateful he finds the strength to get up and come back for cleanup. He kisses me hard as I come down from the euphoria.

"Ryder."

"Too late, Gina. You already said yes."

"I know. It's just… are you sure?"

It's a question I've never asked him.

"As sure as I've ever been."

"How can you be?"

"Because every game when I step out on the field, I have to talk myself out of nerves. Each time I wonder if I'm truly good enough or if it will be the night I fuck it all up."

"You're awesome. You've proven that. Your owner is wrong about you. You will be the next New York Yankees' ace. I know this."

"Maybe." He plants a fast kiss on my mouth before continuing. "One thing I didn't have to talk myself into was you. I look forward to the day you're not only wearing my jersey, but my ring."

I reach for him, but he's moved over to the side of the bed. When he rolls back, he presents me with a box, and I forget to breathe. I've never been the girl who dreamed of a wedding. My heart begins to race as it's opened. The sparkle blinds me and shocks me stupid.

Emotions well out of me and stream down my face. It's gorgeous. I know nothing about diamonds and can only say it's dazzling.

His words distract me. "And you know what's better than having you wearing my jersey and my ring on game night?"

"Me seeing you make history with that famous fastball of yours?" He shakes his head. "What then?"

"You in the stands watching me play with our son or daughter growing inside of you or sitting by your side."

The funny thing is, I can see it, too. When he slides the ring onto my finger, a door opens in my heart, and I eagerly walk through it. I may not have wanted love, but I found it.

"You weren't supposed to stick," I say.

"But I did."

"You did," I admit. "You struck me out with your fastball."

"No, my fastball is nothing compared to when you rounded the bases of my heart after knocking me out the park."

"Baseball analogies, Cowboy?"

"Yep, and you better get used to it."

EPILOGUE

Ryder

My world has come together so nicely, and temporarily, I have two of my favorite women under one roof. The problem I have now is pacifying the third.

"Don't do it," Riley warns.

"What?" I ask innocently. I scrub a hand down my face, pretending not to know what she's talking about. But I do. Gina wants something small. Mom wants everyone we've ever met to attend our wedding.

"Don't choose Mom over your wife."

I'm actually surprised to hear my sister chose Gina over Mom. "You think I would?"

"I see you actually considering whatever she was saying to you on the phone."

I glance at the thing in my hand where I just ended a conversation with my mother.

"What the hell am I supposed to do? She's guilting me by saying I might be the only one of her children to get married," I say, glaring at my twin. I wait for shock to appear on Riley's face, but it doesn't. "Seriously, you told her that?"

She shrugs. "No man will ever be able to deal with me."

"That's because you don't give anyone a chance."

She's never been one to need me to defend her honor growing up. Riley can handle herself. And I may have overheard guys claim she's a lesbian when she doesn't give in to their advances. I might have had a few scrapes that she doesn't know about when I had to set the record straight, not that if she were gay it would be a problem. They, on the other hand, said it like that was a problem. And talking about my sister isn't permitted in my presence. But I've also been there for her when some asshole has broken her heart. It's only happened a few times. Now I think she's given up on dating anyone.

"Stop." She holds up a hand. "Mark's on his way over, so let's end this conversation."

My brow arches. "Mark?" I waggle my eyebrows at her.

"It's not like that. He may help me out of a jam."

"What jam?"

"Well, if you weren't so busy winning the World Series and falling in love, you would know I'm short a caddy and I've been asked to participate in an event for the Make-A-Wish Foundation."

Suddenly, I'm a shitty brother, and I go to apologize. But Riley waves me off and gives me a smile that lets me know I'm forgiven. The doorbell rings, and Riley moves to answer it. That gives me my opportunity to sneak back upstairs. There's someone I left slumbering soundly on my bed.

When I open the door, my future wife sits up, and with no modesty, which I like, lets the sheet slip down her gorgeous body. Her beautiful tits jerk my cock to life. I didn't think it would be possible. We've been fucking nonstop all weekend.

"Are you just going to stand there, Cowboy, and stare at me?"

She has no idea how long I could just look at her and be amazed that she's mine. The fact that she's agreed to marry me and come with me to New York with no conditions feels like I've won the World Series all over again. In fact, we are leaving for New York in a few hours, where I have to meet with the manager while she goes apartment hunting. I would go with her, but we are short on time. She's going to weed out the places she doesn't like. Because I don't care. We could live in a box as long as we are together.

"Is that coffee for me?" she asks, as I continue to stand like a doofus, dumbstruck by her beauty.

Only it's not just her outer layer that has me enthralled. She's told me all her plans, which include a charity that supports kids without families. She wants to make sure kids in foster care aren't forgotten. A lot of money she's inherited has been granted to the state of North Carolina for that purpose. I don't bother to tell her I thought she would sleep in longer, and so the coffee I hold is technically mine. Everything I have is hers, including my first cup of joe in the morning, which I hand over.

She cradles it in her hands as if it's the Holy Grail. The way her eyes roll up reminds me of when she comes. My woman is a super hero and a sexy siren all rolled into one.

"If you continue to look at me like that, I'm going to attack you," she says.

I have to chuckle. She has no idea the things we've yet to do. I haven't told her yet that I want to tie her to the bed spread eagle. I also want to try that swing again, but using it for leverage while I take her ass. It's fast becoming one of her favorite things to do. I can't say that it doesn't turn me the fuck on to know I'm the only one to have had her there.

She's also made me want to beat my chest because she's agreed to stop taking the pill. I can't wait to see her pregnant, so her pussy is always my first mission.

"We can't. Mark is here, and I plan to make you scream," I tease.

Her grin is wicked, and I say *fuck it* to myself. It's my house. Diving for her, the coffee spills some, and I don't care. I'll take my girl any way I can get her, coffee stains or not.

GINA *months later*

"Have you told him yet?" Cassie asks.

I shake my head, unable to speak. I pace the small room. How will I tell him?

She stops me. "It's going to be okay. You look gorgeous."

It will be. Ryder and I have formed a partnership. We've agreed to no secrets. Thus, I can't hold back what I've learned for very long.

I glance down at Cassie's extended belly. "You're going to make a fantastic mother. You know that, don't you?"

"Stop deflecting, Gina. You look perfect. His mouth will be open so wide, the photographer will catch drool."

I laugh while I take a final look in the mirror. The ivory gown I chose is designer, but not couture. Off the rack is what some call it. All the fashion terms I'm learning as the queen of a privately held corporation. It's form-fitted and flares at the calf for a small train. It has cap sleeves and a sweetheart neckline and fits my body perfectly after trying on a half a million gowns with Cassie, Riley, and Ryder's mom for support.

But I don't let her get away with it either. "Don't deflect, Cassie," I mock. "You can't take a compliment. You and Fletcher are going to make great parents."

Her laughs turn to a few tears. She hides them with her hug, which isn't unexpected. I hold on, remembering how just over a year ago, it was us against the world. How things have changed in a short time.

"It's going to be great," she says, just as a knock comes at the door.

Her smile is huge as she greets my father. She gives me a wave before ducking out of the room.

"Are you ready?" he asks.

That's another change in my life. My dad. He's rooted himself in my life, and I find I like him here. He's refused any financial support I offer. But one win is his bitch of a wife is gone, and he tells me he wants to fly solo for a while. Just the fact that he's here is proof that anything can change and for the better.

"I'm glad you're here... Dad."

The word sounds so different now even though it's the same. It tastes sweet and not sour. It's me that dives in for a hug. It's hard not to let the tears spill and ruin my makeup.

"I wouldn't miss it for the world, baby girl."

It's taken us time to get here. We've had many talks where I told him of all his failings. It was something I needed to get off my chest in order for us to find the harmonious place we're in now.

As he escorts me out the door, I have precious moments to reflect. Life threw me several curveballs, but it was Ryder and that damn fastball of his that knocked some sense into me. If not for his persistence, I would still be in a rut. He showed me life's possibilities and opened my eyes and heart to love. Dad and I stand at the opening, and I have a moment to lock eyes with Ryder before the music starts. Mendelssohn's "Wedding March." Who knew I would be a traditional girl? It's surreal how I seem to float toward that beautiful man of mine.

When my dad hands me off, I hear him murmur softly, "Take care of my girl. She's all I have."

Ryder says something I can't make out. Then my hands are in his. Words are foreign to me because I'm caught up in my head, seeing my future, my heart planted with the man I didn't know I'd dreamed of until he showed up in my life.

After we trade vows and exchange I dos, we are pronounced man and wife. Before he kisses me, I tease him.

"You know, now that we're married, I think I'm going to start withholding sex. I only used that as a means to get you."

Then I plant a kiss on him to stop his protest. Teasing me back, he grips my hips and nudges me enough for me to get how much he's not on board with my plan. Our lip-lock grows into something more. That gets us a round of applause and laughter as it lingers longer than appropriate. But when did we ever do anything by the rules?

"You know I'm teasing you, right?" I whisper as we walk. "I married you because you are the best man I know. And you make me a better woman. I love you for that. I love you for you."

Walking back down the aisle, I take in the elaborate setup in the back of the hotel. With lights strung in small trees, the place is magical and sought after for weddings. I wanted a small wedding, but I'd agreed to marry him in

Charlotte.

Logistically, it made sense. Many of Ryder's former teammates as well as his family and friends are in town. The hotel could accommodate the numbers for the location of the wedding and reception in one place. Ryder had suggested Waynesville. And even though it's home, there are too many sad memories for me to be dead set on having it there. Charlotte made more sense.

"You make a beautiful bride, Gina," Ryder's mom says, kissing my cheek and bringing me out of my thoughts.

"Thank you for accepting me into your family."

And they have. Never once have they made me feel like an outsider because I didn't grow up like they did.

Ryder kisses his mother's cheek. "Everyone give us a minute. I would like to spend a few minutes with my wife alone."

That gets a round of cheers and good nature catcalls from some. Ryder's entire family is here, including Fletcher and his parents. His brother, Chase, even shows up. He's in town for a few weeks before he flies back out of the country. We haven't seen him since the Cougars won the pennant. He, however, doesn't seem entirely here. And he only got into town this morning, so I haven't had a chance to talk to him. What I do know is that he's made a name for himself in the world of European soccer.

Ryder doesn't take me inside the house. Instead, we head for the room that had been designated for me to get dressed in. Slipping inside, we make it just inside the door before his mouth is on mine. Before I can lose myself in his touch, I pull back.

"Wait, I need to tell you something."

"Talk later. I need you right now. That dress…"

When he has a fist full of fabric bunched at my thigh, a knock precedes the door opening, and Fletcher pokes his head in. "I saw you guys head in this direction. The photographer wants you out here."

Ryder groans. "Remind me again why I made you my best man."

Fletcher only grins. We follow him back into the fray. Once we get to the bridal part for pictures, Riley gives me a look, knowing what Fletcher broke up.

"Congratulations, sister-in-law," Riley says.

She's gorgeous and oblivious to Mark's prolonged gazes. The guy has it bad. I have a bit of nostalgia as I remember when he looked at me that way. However, I'm ecstatic for him. Riley reminds me of myself. But she's a Wilde. And something tells me, she's more of a romantic than she thinks she is.

It isn't until the photographer takes us aside that I finally have a quiet moment with my husband.

"Wife," he says.

Butterflies rush through me. Something about knowing we are truly and well married makes me feel girlish as heat rushes to my cheek. "Husband."

"No kissing," the photographer admonishes as Ryder is about to do just that. "Only a few more."

As the man sets up the shot, I whisper, "I'm pregnant."

The picture of Ryder's face will turn out to be one of my favorites. It's comical how large his eyes get and somehow with perfect timing, it is captured forever.

Ryder will never say it, but I think he wanted us to have a kid close in age to Fletcher and Cassie's impending bundle. He wants our kids to have the bond he and Fletcher had before his family moved to the other side of the country.

And even though we settled on a place in New York I insisted on paying for, because as I told Ryder we are partners, he's convinced me for us to make Waynesville our home base. My father and grandparents are there. And Fletcher and Cassidy have a house there. So we are scouting locations of land for us to build something. And maybe a lot large enough for me to build something for my dad, too. Riley will keep the condo once we have our place built. So Fletcher and Cassidy will be close.

The apartment we selected in Manhattan is grand, but it's kind of hard not to find something a little over the top that has the security we will need now that Ryder will no doubt be a superstar. We have sweeping views of Central Park and the Hudson River. I've never lived in a high-rise, and it should be interesting. My biological mom's company headquarters are there as well, so I'll have time to spend learning the business when Ryder is playing his game.

Our future looks bright, and even brighter with all

the changes in our life.

Ryder says, "Who's Sam's date?"

"I don't know her name, but I plan to find out."

Sam brought a woman with him. I watch them in the distance. I think about the business venture I formed with Sam to buy into the business and give the Dirty Hammer some much-needed upgrades. It's weird not working there full-time anymore. And if I'm honest, I'm so ready to be a mom. So ready to be the best parent I can be, along with being an amazing wife. It will be a new adventure.

I wrap myself in Ryder's arms, ignoring the protest of the photographer.

"You've got me so hard," he whispers into my ear.

I giggle, which catches me off guard for a second. "You're always hard."

"That's you fault," he teases.

"I wouldn't have it any other way."

"Which is why you're going to stay pregnant. Soon we will have a little league formed by our children."

"You're crazy." I laugh.

"It's true, and we are going to make amazing parents."

"We are," I agree.

"But first, I'm going to take my beautiful wife to Tuscany."

"Tuscany?" He hadn't told me where we were going for our honeymoon.

"Absolutely. We have a private villa with a pool and a

view. I'm going to make love to you all day and all night, so forget sightseeing."

"Is that so?"

"Then we'll come back in time to see our godchild born."

"What about me visiting the headquarters of my company?"

I hadn't gone to Italy. I did go to the New York offices of my company, which still seems weird to think it. I've never been out of the country. I decided I wanted to share that experience with someone and not alone. And only one person did I have in mind. My husband.

"We'll fit that in somehow." He laughs.

Cassie is ready to pop, which is evident by her maternity matron of honor dress.

"Uh huh. Then what?"

"Then I'll watch my son grow in your belly."

I raise a brow. "Son?"

"Of course."

"Okay, so I won't shatter your dreams yet that we're having a girl."

"Not going to happen. Though I would love a little girl that looks like her mother."

Damn, if he doesn't look at me like I am Miss Universe holding the key to his heart. And what a daunting thing that would be if I didn't love him just as much.

"Since you are so sure, what is the first thing you're going to teach our son?"

"That's easy."

"Tell me then."

"I'll share with him the secret to how we Wilde baseball players throw a fastball."

THE END

A THANK YOU

We'd like to thank you for taking the time out of your busy life to read our novel. Above all we hope you loved it. If you did, we would love it back if you could spare just a few more minutes to leave a review on your favorite retailer. If you do, could you be so kind and not leave any spoilers about the story? Thanks so much!

ACKNOWLEDGEMENTS

To every athlete out there, who dedicates hours and hours to their sport, we thank you and appreciate you. Not only do you entertain us, but you also give us something to write (fantasize) about!

To our readers: you guys are THE BEST! And we say that from the bottoms of our hearts. We love and appreciate each and every one of you and we hope our little dirty, flirty romance is something that you love. We decided to play a little with this and veer away from the serious so we could have some fun. So please tell us what you think. Hit us up on Facebook or wherever, but there will be more Wilde Players on the way.

Here are the lovely people we'd like to say THANK YOU to. Our beta readers: Kristie, Andrea, Nina, and Jill. You ladies are our shining stars and always make our books brighter and prettier than they can ever have been without you. We Love you to the end zone and then some!

Thank you Nina Grinstead, and Social Butterfly PR for running your butt off in getting our stuff out there when we were so late. We love you!

And thank you Rick Miles at Redcoat PR For everything, but especially for putting up with Annie (and Walter) after two pots of coffee. Next time she'll just give the coffee to Walter.

ABOUT THE AUTHORS

A.M. HARGROVE

One day, on her way home from work as a sales manager, USA Today bestselling author, A. M. Hargrove, realized her life was on fast forward and if she didn't do something soon, it would be too late to write that work of fiction she had been dreaming of her whole life. So she made a quick decision to quit her job and reinvented herself as a Naughty and Nice Romance Author.

Annie fancies herself all of the following: Reader, Writer, Dark Chocolate Lover, Ice Cream Worshipper, Coffee Drinker (swears the coffee, chocolate, and ice cream should be added as part of the USDA food groups), Lover of Grey Goose (and an extra dirty martini), #WalterThePuppy Lover, and if you're ever around her for more than five minutes, you'll find out she's a non-stop talker. Other than loving writing about romance, she loves hanging out with her family and binge watching TV with her husband. You can find out more about her books at http://www.amhargrove.com.

TERRI E. LAINE

Terri E. Laine, USA Today bestselling author, left a lucrative career as a CPA to pursue her love for writing. Outside of her roles as a wife and mother of three, she's always been a dreamer and an avid reader at a young age.

Many years later, she got a crazy idea to write a novel and set out to try to publish it. With over a dozen titles published under various pen names, the rest is history. Her journey has been a blessing, and a dream realized. She looks forward to many more memories to come.

You can find more about her books at www.terrielaine.com.

STALK TERRI E. LAINE

If you would like more information about me, sign up for my newsletter at http://eepurl.com/bDJ9kb. I love to hear from my readers.

www.terrielaine.com

Facebook Page: /TerriELaineAuthor

Facebook: /TerriELaineBooks

Instagram @terrielaineauthor

Twitter @TerriLaineBooks

Goodreads:/ Terri_E_Laine

Other Books by Terri E. Laine

Cruel & Beautiful

A Mess of a Man

A Beautiful Sin

Chasing Butterflies

STALK A.M. HARGROVE

If you would like to hear more about what's going on in my world, please subscribe to my mailing list at http://amhargrove.com/mailing-list/.

Please stalk me. I'll love you forever if you do. Seriously.

Website: www.amhargrove.com

Twitter: @ amhargrove1

Facebook Page:/ AMHargroveAuthor

Facebook:/ anne.m.hargrove

Goodreads:/ amhargrove1

Instagram: @ amhargroveauthor

Pinterest:/ amhargrove1

annie@amhargrove.com

OTHER BOOKS BY A. M. HARGROVE

Cruel and Beautiful
A Mess of A Man
A Beautiful Sin

The Guardians of Vesturon Series:
Survival, Book 1
Resurrection, Book 2
Determinant, Book 3
reEmergent, Book 4
Dark Waltz, A Praestani Novel
Death Waltz, A Praestani Novel

The Edge Series:
Edge of Disaster
Shattered Edge
Kissing Fire

The Tragic Series:
Tragically Flawed, Tragic 1
Tragic Desires, Tragic 2

The Hart Brothers Series:
Freeing Her, Book 1
Freeing Him, Book 2
Kestrel, Book 3
The Fall and Rise of Kade Hart

Other Standalone Novels:
Sabin, A Seven Novel
Exquisite Betrayal
Dirty Nights, The Novel

44313856R10146

Made in the USA
Middletown, DE
03 June 2017